Bestselling author Merryn Allingham was born into an army family and spent her childhood on the move. Unsurprisingly, it gave her itchy feet, and in her twenties she escaped an unloved secretarial career to work as cabin crew and see the world. The arrival of marriage, children and cats meant a more settled life in the south of England, where she's lived ever since. Having gained a PhD, she taught university literature for many years and loved every minute of it. What could be better than spending one's life reading and talking about books? Well, writing them perhaps.

Six Regency period romances followed, then those itchy feet kicked in. The Regency was abandoned and *Daisy's War*, a wartime trilogy, found its way to the top of the Amazon charts, followed by the Summerhayes books—a saga of romance and intrigue set in the Sussex countryside during the summers of 1914 and 1944.

But itchy feet never rest and in 2020 she finally went over to the dark side! The crime series, the Tremayne Mysteries, is set in locations around the world and features Nancy, a feisty 1950s heroine, turned amateur sleuth.

Keep in touch with Merryn via the web:

Website: **https://www.merrynallingham.com**

Facebook: **http://www.facebook.com/MerrynWrites**

Twitter: **http://www.twitter.com/merrynwrites**

## *Other Books in this Series*

*The Dangerous Promise (2020)*

*Venetian Vendetta (2020)*

*Caribbean Evil (2020)*

*Cornish Requiem (2021)*

*Rio Revenge (2021)*

# THE LONDON RECKONING

Merryn Allingham

# THE LONDON RECKONING

This novel is entirely a work of fiction. The names, characters and incidents portrayed in it are the work of the author's imagination. Any resemblance to actual persons, living or dead, events or localities is entirely coincidental.

First published in Great Britain 2021 by The Verrall Press

Cover art: Berni Stevens Book Cover Design

# *Chapter One*

**London, January, 1958**

*Man that is born of woman hath but a short time to live …he fleeth as it were a shadow… thou knowest, Lord, the secrets of our hearts…*

Standing by the graveside, Nancy Tremayne allowed the words to flow—over, above, around her. A torrent of words, disjointed, ungraspable. Her mind tried to catch at the phrases, hold on to them as though they might tether her to a world made newly strange. The secrets of her heart? She hardly knew them any more, not with the husband, who had loved and protected her, lying only feet away.

The coffin of polished mahogany was being lifted by six bearers onto a canvas webbing. Could Leo really be in there? She gazed blindly at the men standing either side of the gaping hole. Perran, she knew Perran, if not the others. Leo's brother had arrived at Cavendish Street last night in almost as big a daze as Nancy. How could this have happened, they'd said to each other, hunched over the fire Mrs Brindley, the housekeeper, had made for them. How could it have happened to a man not yet fifty years old?

Perry looked old, Nancy thought dispassionately, his face haggard, his figure stooped. Leo's death had decimated him. And who was that beside Perry, taking the strain of the holding straps as the coffin began its journey down into the grave? Leo's temporary assistant? Yes, it was Dominic Gray. Temporary because her husband had never truly accepted that Archie had left. Losing Archie Jago had been a major blow and though Gray always appeared to be as efficient as he was smart—his regulation black raincoat cut more sharply than most—her husband had never settled into the relationship. In the circumstances, it was good of Dominic to take on the role of bearer.

*We therefore commit his body to the ground; earth to earth, ashes to ashes, dust to dust; in sure and certain hope of the Resurrection to eternal life, through our Lord Jesus Christ.*

The sound of earth hitting wood brought Nancy out of her trance. Her stomach was so tightly knotted she could hardly breathe. This was it. This was really happening. Leo was dead. Gone. And she was once more alone in the world.

She felt a hand at her elbow and turned to see Mrs Brindley's concerned face. The woman had never made Nancy feel welcome at Cavendish Street, not from the moment she'd walked through its front door, nor through the years she'd been married to Leo. These last few days, however, the housekeeper had been uncharacteristically gentle.

'We should go, my dear,' Mrs Brindley said. 'There's no wake to cope with and you can be quiet once we're home. I'll put the kettle on as soon as we're back.' She glanced across at Perry, looking lost among the crowd. 'Mr Perran will be coming with us,' she said with certainty. 'There's nothing to keep him here.'

There were plenty of people to know. The parish church was a large building, but every pew had been packed. Even the two galleries high up on each wall had been filled with mourners, some having travelled long distances to attend. The size of the congregation was a testatment to Leo's reputation as an expert in Renaissance art. Not only that—a testament to his work as a valued colleague and a friend. From her pew, Nancy had glimpsed several of the managers from Abingers, the auction house where she'd once worked as a lowly assistant, where she and Leo had first met. Mr Harker, Mr Simmonds, she saw. Drab, grey figures on a drab grey day.

The clouds had been banking from the moment she'd left Cavendish Street, and were far darker now and louring overhead. A soft drizzle began to fall and Mrs Brindley opened her large, black umbrella to hold it high above their heads. They'd turned to walk to the lych gate, when a short, plumpish woman hurried towards them.

'Nancy, I am so sorry,' she said breathlessly.

From beneath the voluminous umbrella, Nancy made out a well-known face. Her mentor from the studio where she'd been an apprentice.

'I knew Leo was unwell,' Connie said, 'but I'd no idea...' her voice trailed off.

'It's been a shock for all of us.' Nancy was surprised she could form the words.

'You mustn't think of coming back to work. Take your time and ring me when you feel ready.'

Connie was a dear, so supportive, so wonderfully knowledgeable on art restoration. She had steered Nancy through three years of apprenticeship and, just as her best pupil—or so Connie always maintained—had gained her final qualification and begun work as a fully fledged restorer, Leo's illness had become too serious for Nancy to continue.

'I'll be back very soon,' she promised. 'Returning to work will be good for me.'

'Just as long as you know there's no rush.' Connie squeezed her hand before she, too, turned to make her way out of the churchyard.

Out of the churchyard and back to the studio, Nancy thought, that's where Connie would be going. Back to a life that hadn't changed. Like all these other people, drifting slowly towards the gate. Life goes on—it was a trite saying, but a true one.

Ahead, a gap opened between the mass of dark gaberdines and, for an instant, Nancy saw a flash of colour. Rose, it was Rose, her very best friend, wearing a pink scarf, a small flag of happiness on a sorrowful day. She must have come all the way from Dorset to be here, bless her, and hadn't said a word. Nancy excused herself to Mrs Brindley and walked swiftly over to her friend. Rose held out her arms to her.

'How good of you!' Nancy said, emerging from a warm embrace. 'But why didn't you tell me you were making the journey? You could have stayed with me at the house.'

'I wanted to come,' Rose said simply, 'I wanted to be here, but I didn't want to put you to any trouble. You've enough to cope with—this is such a terrible day—and the journey was easy enough. I came up on the early train and I've one going back in an hour.'

'I wish you could stay.'

Nancy held on to her friend's hand. She hadn't seen Rose for months. They had been writing, but she had managed only a single visit to Dorset shortly after she and Leo returned from Brazil, and Rose had never made it to London as they'd planned.

'I'll come and stay soon,' Rose promised. 'When I've arranged things with Mike. The girls are quite sensible now, but they still need a grown-up around.'

'Of course. But you will come?'

'I will. And *you* must come to Dorset again. Same spare room, I'm afraid. Nothing as palatial as your townhouse, but you survived it last time!'

'And I will again,' she said, kissing Rose goodbye. 'I'll write soon.'

For someone who had spent years in her parents' small bungalow or her own scrubby bedsitter, any spare room was palatial. Cavendish Street might be a large house, but it was one Nancy had never got used to.

Turning to see that Perry had joined Mrs Brindley, his duty as a pall bearer done, Nancy went over to him.

She tucked her arm in his. 'Time to go?'

'I'll find a taxi,' he said, his face ravaged with sadness. 'Mrs Brindley, you'll come with us?'

As they moved off in the direction of the lych gate, he pointed to the mass of wreaths, arranged in a double bank beside the brick path. 'What a display—truly magnificent!'

The flowers *were* magnificent, though the expensive wreaths sent by Leo's clients left Nancy indifferent. It was the smaller, more intimate posies she bent to examine. The white roses she'd ordered were there, a small bouquet from Mrs Brindley and—she knew the writing—Archie had sent snowdrops and white anemones. While Perry and the housekeeper walked ahead, she bent down and, on impulse, tugged the label loose. Slightly shamefaced, she secreted it in her handbag.

Hoping no one had seen, she walked swiftly along the path—until she reached the wreath at the end of the line. She stared hard at the card attached to its inner ring, momentarily paralysed. She knew *this* handwriting, too. Philip March, the man who had stalked her for years. The man who had tried to kill her. The wreath meant he knew Leo was dead, but what did it mean for her? Was it to give notice that March was back in her life and ready to cause harm, or simply that he was sorry her husband had died and the flowers marked the closing of a chapter? No, not that. Definitely, not that. Her body, her mind, her heart, shrieked that it was a warning.

'Are you coming, Mrs Tremayne?' Mrs Brindley had come to a halt and was looking back at her.

'Yes,' she said quickly, trying to blot the name of March from her mind, and hurrying to join her companions.

Before they could pass through the lych gate, they found themelves beseiged by people eager to offer their condolences but, knowing hardly anyone who approached her, Nancy found conversation difficult. It was evident, too, that some were feeling cheated. They had expected a wake to follow, a gathering of some kind, to celebrate Leo's life.

She had been adamant, though, that a church service was all she could face and her brother-in-law had backed her wishes. She hadn't wanted to hear over and over again how wonderful Leo was and what a loss to the art world he'd be, when all she could think of was what his loss meant to her. There would be a memorial service later, she told anyone who enquired. Much later and held in Cornwall, where Leo truly belonged. She owed that at least to his father, who had been too infirm to travel to London. There had been a tussle with Ned Tremayne as to where his son should be buried, but as Leo's wife, Nancy had won. She'd wanted Leo close, a grave she could sit by, take flowers to. Not a grave hundreds of miles away in a county she rarely visited.

The rain had intensified, no longer drizzle, but a steady downpour. A freezing mist had slid from the clouds and blanketed whole swathes of the churchyard, the lichen-strewn gravestones disappearing into its smothering greyness. The trees dripped rain steadily from already soaked branches. A true day for a funeral, she thought. But hadn't every day these last few months been as grey? Christmas had been forgotten, New Year, too. And now in the second week of January, the rest of the winter stretched ahead, a cold, dismal blank. She gave herself an inner shake. She must guard against such self-pity. It was the months of sickness, the months of worry, that had worn her down. And now this—a quiet death when no one, not even the doctors, had been expecting it.

While they waited for Perry to find a cab, Dominic Gray came up to her, raising his hat beneath his umbrella and, for a moment, touching her arm in a gesture of sympathy.

'The cab's here,' Perry said, appearing at her shoulder.

She nodded a goodbye to Gray, at the same time thanking him for his help, and walked through the church gate to the waiting taxi. For an instant only, she looked back at the still open grave. She was leaving Leo alone, in the cold and the dark and the wet. It was so very hard. She frowned. A figure was standing by the grave. A lone mourner, but a figure she knew. Archie Jago. She had thought Archie would telephone or at least write when he heard of Leo's death, but there had been only silence. Archie had made a vow to walk away, and it seemed he was intent on keeping it, even in death. Yet, not absolutely. He'd sent flowers, he'd come to the funeral, sat unknown and unseen in the shadows of the church, not wanting to meet her, not wanting to speak. He'd come for Leo, and she must be glad of that.

## Chapter Two

Sitting in the taxi, between Mrs Brindley and her brother-in-law, Nancy was fairly sure that neither of them had seen Archie at the graveside. Perry knew him from their home village of Port Madron, of course, and would have insisted that Archie came back to Cavendish Street for tea. She was glad that hadn't happened, though she doubted the housekeeper would have seconded the invitation. Mrs Brindley and Archie had always had a brisk relationship. Nancy allowed herself a faint smile, recalling the various small spats she'd witnessed between them over the years.

'It was quite a congregation,' Perry said at last trying, Nancy thought, to break the heavy silence that had fallen.

'Mr Leo was a great man,' the housekeeper said proudly, 'and a good man. He had plenty of friends as well as colleagues.' As though she wasn't sure her audience had registered the point, she added, 'Mr Leo was highly valued and he'll be sorely missed.'

After that homily, the silence returned, and was only broken again when they reached Cavendish Street.

'I'll get a train back to Truro the day after tomorrow, if that's okay with you,' Perry told her, as they walked up the gleaming white steps to the front door.

'You won't stay longer?' Nancy wasn't sure whether

she was regretful or glad to have the house to herself. Mrs Brindley didn't live in, but came daily to clean, shop and cook.

'I can't leave Dad for more than a few days,' Perry said. 'Leo… it's knocked him for six, and he wasn't that strong before. He's never really been his old self since the heart attack.'

'Grace is looking after him, though?'

'Yes, bless her. She's actually moved in while I'm away. Fortunately—for me, at least—the *Morwenna* is laid up for repairs this week, and Richard Jago won't be going to sea. It's meant Grace could leave the girls to their father's tender care, and devote herself to Dad.'

'She's a gem.'

'She is and I can't thank you enough, Nancy, for suggesting I offer her the job. Dad loves her. I couldn't have foreseen that. At best, I thought he'd tolerate her presence in the house, because he knew someone had to look after him when I'm at the mine all day. But he loves her. Grace brings him all the village gossip and I bring him all the news from Wheal Agnes, so he's well entertained.'

In the hall, Mrs Brindley shook her umbrella and slotted it into the bentwood stand. 'Go and sit down,' she said, shooing them towards an open doorway. 'I'll be in shortly with a tray of tea.'

Nancy walked into the sitting room, feeling as though each step was a mountain to climb. How ridiculous to be so weary, when all she'd done was sit in a cold church and stand by a cold grave. The rain was hammering against the French doors and she swished the long velour curtains together, shutting out the miserable day beyond, then sunk into the deep cushions of Leo's favourite chair.

'It's been a shock and no denying it.' Perry gave an audible sigh, slumping onto the sofa, his legs outstretched. 'I knew

Leo was ill. Knew about his breathing problems and the bronchitis, but I… we… had no idea.'

'It turned into more than bronchitis. That was always a danger once winter arrived, but I'd hoped he'd built up enough strength during the year to fight it.'

'You did get some sunshine. We had a postcard from Italy—Lake Maggiore, wasn't it?'

Nancy nodded wistfully. 'We spent a lovely few weeks there in June. No work, just lazy sauntering and browsing any galleries we could find. Eating well, too. Leo hired a villa with its own cook! It was truly relaxing and his health improved hugely. He looked so well afterwards. Perhaps too well,' she said thoughtfully.

Perry straightened himself. 'What do you mean?'

'He promised me he'd reduce his workload—when we were in Brazil and he was recouperating from being attacked in Rio—but when we got back from Italy, stuff started to arrive in bulk and he simply wouldn't say no. He said he was well enough, and I shouldn't fuss. One project after another, one talk after another. He found the exhibition Abingers asked him to curate a complete nightmare—pictures not arriving, the insurance being messed up, then the publicity went out at the wrong time and Aubrey Simmonds was wringing his hands that no one would attend and the firm would lose money. The practicalities were nothing to do with Leo—his job was to select the paintings and detail where and how they were hung—but you know what a perfectionist he is… was. He found it very stressful.'

'It sounds it. I would think Abingers would have been more thoughtful.'

'It wasn't their fault, to be honest. Leo behaved as though he was fully fit when really he was still recovering from several winters of being ill. And Archie wasn't here to tell him to stop.'

'I'm sorry he lost Archie Jago. Surprised, too. I thought the chap really enjoyed working for Leo. Grace was a bit surprised, too, well the whole Jago family, I suppose, though Morwenna didn't say much.'

Morwenna wouldn't, Nancy thought. Archie's mother would have known immediately what had prompted her son to leave a well-paid job with a boss he'd known for much of his life. Morwenna would have known that it was Nancy. Nancy's fault that Archie, having already moved out of Cavendish Street, was now severing his last link with the Tremaynes, believing he couldn't stay working for a man he liked and respected. Not when he was deeply in love with that man's wife.

'Leo did employ somone else,' Nancy said hastily. 'He was at the church today. One of your fellow pall bearers, in fact—Dominic Gray. You saw him at the church gate, saying goodbye. Leo met him at Abingers and managed to negotiate for Dominic to work part of the week at the auction house and part of the week for him.'

'Was he any good?'

'Good enough, but Leo was never really easy with him.'

It was more that he missed his old assistant so badly, Nancy thought, remembering how Archie's absence had eaten away at her husband. 'It put more stress on Leo when he didn't need it. What with that, and the huge workload he took on, he wasn't fit to fight bronchitis when it came calling again.'

Perry's face set in deep lines. 'We knew he was pretty poorly. Dad wanted you both at Penleven for Christmas, but I persuaded him that Leo was best staying here and not travelling in the cold. We both thought he was getting better, though.'

'So did I. He went downhill very quickly. Before I knew it, bronchitis had turned into pneumonia and he was whisked into hospital. Two days later, he...' her voice faltered... 'he was dead.'

Perry reached out for her hand and held it gently. 'It must have been dreadful for you, Nancy, being so completely alone.'

There was a pause and he seemed to be debating whether to say what was in his mind. In the end, he began tentatively. 'Your parents? I know they're still alive, but couldn't they...'

'No.' Even to Nancy's ears, she sounded harsh. 'They've heard about Leo—they sent a card and no doubt a wreath. But I don't see them and it's better that way.'

Perry knew nothing about her mother and father, the history that lay between them. Nancy would never forgive the betrayal she'd suffered at their hands, the fact they'd delivered their daughter into the hands of a monster. They had been mistaken, true, taken in by a smooth-tongued imposter, but they had wanted her to marry Philip March so badly they'd chosen to ignore her fears, to ignore her pleas for help. Wanted it so badly, they were prepared to risk their daughter's life. She had no wish to see them. Not again. Not ever.

'Here we are.' Mrs Brindley marched briskly through the doorway, carrying a laden tray. Pushing aside a pile of art magazines, she settled it on the mosaic-topped table.

'I've brought a plate of madeleines, too. They were made yesterday. You should try to eat something.' She looked directly at Nancy. 'And there's a casserole in the fridge. Just pop it into the oven for your suppers, and I'll be back tomorrow.'

'Thank you, Mrs Brindley.' She felt an unusual warmth for the housekeeper. It might not be long before she turned back into the sharp-tongued woman Nancy had always known, but these last few days she had been a store of strength.

Perry poured two cups of tea and sat back on the sofa. A loud click from the hall signalled that Mrs Brindley had left for home.

'It's too early, I suppose, to think about the future,' he said. 'Work and so on.'

'I spoke to Connie at the funeral. She was my mentor at the studio—we'd only been working as colleagues for a few months when I had to give up, but she's such a kind woman. She tells me I must forget work for as long as I need to. It's ironic, really.' Nancy eyes were sad. 'It's what Leo always wanted. We'd agreed—Leo and I—that we'd both work less and be together more, though in the end it didn't happen.'

'Because Leo chose to forget the agreement?' Her brother-in-law's face wore a sympathetic smile.

She had no wish to go into detail, the desire to reconnect with each other, to try and be husband and wife again after weeks of estrangement. She was unsure if Leo had ever spoken to his brother about the odd marriage he'd made, but Nancy was certain Perry wouldn't want to talk about it, even if he knew why or how they'd married.

'After we got back from Italy, we hardly saw each other, despite my working fewer hours,' she said briefly. 'Still, when he fell ill this last autumn, not being in full-time work was a godsend.'

'And now?'

'I'm going back to the studio,' she said decidedly. 'Probably earlier than Connie expects, and probably full-time. I think it will help.'

Perry nodded. 'It should. I know when I've had a problem—when Dad had that sudden heart attack, though you can't compare the two—I found being at Wheal Agnes, talking to the miners, sorting out day-to-day business, took my mind off the awfulness of the situation.'

Nancy leaned over and picked up the plate. 'Mrs B makes a mean madeleine. Please have one.'

'Only if you do.'

Reluctantly, she took a cake and bit into it. It felt strange in her mouth as though she'd never eaten before. But Mrs Brindley was right. She had to eat. These last few months, she'd lost weight and she'd been too slender to begin with. She had to eat to keep herself fit. There were decisions to make.

As if reading her thoughts, Perry asked, 'What will you do about the house?'

## *Chapter Three*

'I'll have to sell.' It was a bald statement. 'The house is too big for me. Really, it's too big for two people, but Leo loved it.'

'And you don't,' he said perceptively.

'It's a beautiful house, but… something smaller, I think,' she ended lightly. 'And something that doesn't cost a small fortune to run.'

'Leo left you all right, though?' Worry lines appeared on Perry's forehead.

'I imagine so. I don't know the details of the will, but in any case my salary is nothing like Leo's and I'd have to move eventually. The house is just too expensive. And better to go when I choose rather than be forced to sell in a hurry.'

Perry took a sip of tea. 'That sounds sensible, but it's sad you have to sell. It is a beautiful house.' He gave a long sigh. 'You know, Nancy, you can always come down to Cornwall. I know your work is here, but there'll be a home for you at Penleven, if you want it.'

'Thank you, Perry. I'll remember.'

Perran Tremayne was a dear. He'd tried so hard to make her feel welcome in the family—unlike his father. She had been a disappointment to Ned. In Ned Tremayne's eyes, his brilliant younger son had been mad to marry a nobody, and he had never let Nancy forget it. Even now, after losing that brilliant son, he would be as brusque as ever the next time she walked through the door of Penleven. But she wouldn't be doing that until she had to. She'd never felt comfortable there. Ned's attitude was one thing, but the house itself made her uneasy, and the attacks she'd suffered when Philip March once more erupted into her world, had made the place less inviting still.

How had Philip learned of her husband's death? It wouldn't be difficult, she supposed. He could have read the obituary she'd been forced to publish, or maybe her father had read it and been keen to relay the news to her erstwhile fiancé. The man who had stalked and threatened her until Leo had ridden to her rescue with an offer of marriage. The man who had tracked her down to Cornwall and nearly killed her. If it hadn't been for Archie…

But she wouldn't think of Archie, wouldn't think of that visit to Cornwall. Neither of them wanted to remember their betrayal of Leo, but neither of them could forget. In the end, it had prompted Archie to walk out of his job and cut the last link he had with her.

He'd come to the funeral today. Paying his respects, that was the phrase. Mourning a man that in his own way he'd loved, a man whose life he'd saved in a war that was now becoming distant. Archie had made no attempt to approach her, to speak to her, and that's the way it must stay. The well of guilt was too deep.

'I'll wash up,' Perry said, jolting her from her reverie, 'and maybe you should rest before supper.' He picked up the tray, making for the doorway. 'I must give Penleven a ring and see how Grace is coping, but have a lie down for a while. You don't look well.'

Nancy got up from the chair, her limbs feeling old and

aching, and caught sight of her face in the oval mirror that hung above the painted wood mantelpiece. Pale, certainly. Almost ghostly, as though she had ceased to exist along with Leo. Perhaps, after all, if she had been able to speak to Archie... He gave her strength. Or had done. She wondered where he was right now, what he was doing, what he was thinking.

*

Archie walked all the way home from Marylebone to the East End. He'd planned to get a bus but, glimpsing Nancy at the church gate, he'd felt the need to be on the move, his feet pounding the pavements, an echo of a heartbeat that wouldn't quieten. He'd known it was foolish to go to the funeral, but he'd felt he had no other option. The flowers he'd sent weren't enough—he couldn't let Leo be buried without some kind of observance. Trusting he could attend without being noticed, he'd deliberately sat at the rear of the church, half-hidden in the shadows and, when the mourners had trickled out into the churchyard, he'd hung back until they left the graveside. Not long enough, it seemed. Perran Tremayne and Mrs Brindley were at the church gate, and with them, Nancy.

He'd not spoken to her for nearly a year. Not seen her, at least not officially. One day last autumn, when falling leaves and bare branches had him succumb to a melancholy he couldn't shake, he'd walked past the studio where Nancy worked. It was a basement premises and from the pavement there was a clear view of the restorers at work. She'd been sitting by the window and he'd allowed himself a brief glance. Absorbed in what looked an intricate piece of painting, taking small, meticulous strokes of the brush, she seemed calm, content. It had made him feel good to know that, but also empty.

Life *was* pretty empty. He'd managed to get clerical work here and there, often on a temporary basis, and been offered a permanent post at the last firm he'd worked for. But he couldn't settle and he'd refused it. He'd even considered going back to Cornwall, but there was nothing at Port Madron except Ma and his brother and family. No work except gutting fish. It would have been an admission of defeat to go back, and Ma, at least, would know why he was doing it. He hated the thought of anyone knowing how he felt, even his mother. It was too private, too painful.

The trip to Rio last February had decided him. He'd been reluctant to make the journey, but Nancy's telegram that Leo was in hospital and needed him had forced his hand. His boss had made a decent enough recovery, at least at the time, but after that trip, he'd known this itch—be honest, it was no itch—this longing for Nancy, was never going away.

He'd already left his comfortable flat in the Cavendish Street house for a tiny space in the East End, thinking that surely with distance between them, it would be okay, but while he worked for Leo, it was never going to be okay. Rio had taught him that. The only decent thing to do was find another job and, seeing Nancy today, he knew he'd been right. She had looked so fragile, so filled with sadness, that he'd wanted to rush across the churchyard and hold her tight. It was the one thing he couldn't do. She was a free woman now, he realised, but there was a whole mountain of regret, of guilt, of lies, between them. There was Leo between them and he'd always be there.

A month or so ago, Archie had bumped into Mrs Brindley in the West End. He hardly ever went up West, but he'd needed some shoes and could find nothing to fit in Blackmans, his usual shop in Cheshire Street. The old girl had actually seemed pleased to see him—that was a turn up for the book—

and she'd told him then that Leo had developed bronchitis again. *Too much work,* she'd said severely. *Mr Leo needs a strong hand to stop him taking on so much. You shouldn't have left. That Dominic Gray is a bit too smooth for my liking. A 'yes' man, if you know what I mean.*

This afternoon, Archie had picked him out straightaway and silently agreed with Mrs B. Dominic Gray was more than "a bit too smooth". At the time, he'd not said much to the housekeeper, just that he hoped Leo would soon be on the mend. His boss—even now he thought of Leo as his boss—had been plagued by bronchitis these last few winters. Ma always said he'd got the weakness from his mother. Rachel Tremayne had died prematurely from a virulent lung infection when Leo was only sixteen and, when the doctors in Rio diagnosed pulmonary fibrosis—at times, an inherited disease—it seemed that Ma had been right. It meant that Leo's lungs could only get worse.

Still, it had been a shock when, a week or so ago Perran Tremayne had called, white-faced, at his mother's cottage. Archie had been in Cornwall for Christmas, was in fact about to pack his suitcase to return to London, when Perry arrived on their doorstep, hardly able to speak for grief. Leo was dead. Archie could hardly believe it, but when Perry telephoned him later in London to tell him the date and time of the funeral, he was forced to. That open grave today had brought a new, painful reality.

By the time he turned into Reardon Road, Archie's feet were hurting badly. Blisters, damn it, he thought. That's new shoes for you. He'd get a bowl of warm water and soak his feet. Then a beer from the small fridge he'd treated himself to, and some bread and cheese. He hadn't been sure if there'd be a funeral breakfast, or whatever it was called, but he wouldn't have gone in any case, and it was clear there wasn't when he saw Perry hailing a taxi, ready to shepherd the small group back to Cavendish Street.

What would Nancy do when she got there, he wondered? How was she coping with such sudden loss? Not well, by the look of it. Letting himself into the small upstairs flat he now called home, Archie was swept by an overwhelming sense of hollowness. Here he was, still alive and well, while Leo lay alone in the churchyard.

## *Chapter Four*

Two days later, Nancy waved her brother-in-law off from Paddington station on his way back to Truro. Perry hadn't wanted to leave her alone, but it was clear he'd been anxious to return home. Ned Tremayne was doing well, according to Grace Jago, but missing his son. And work, too, needed Perry's attention. Francisco Silva, the new owner of Wheal Agnes, had written of his great sadness at the news of Leo's death, and sent one of the enormous caskets of flowers that Nancy had seen at the church. But business was business and Senhor Silva was eager to speak to Perran in his office. Something to do with the new under-sea extension, Grace thought, which though incomplete, was already producing tin of a better quality. The mine was at last beginning to turn a profit.

Leo's death would change nothing at Wheal Agnes. Francisco would still be the owner, Perry the manager, and that would continue until Perry retired. Nothing had changed in Cornwall, but everything had changed in Cavendish Street. Nancy took a taxi back from the station—an extravagence she thought was allowable—and ran down the stairs to see Mrs Brindley, busy in the kitchen as always.

Shrugging off her thick winter coat, Nancy was quick with her thanks. 'That was a lovely chicken you roasted for us yesterday.'

Mrs Brindley looked up, dusting flour from her hands. 'And this will be a lovely steak and kidney pie. Mind you eat it tonight!'

'I will, I promise. I thought I'd work in Mr Leo's study this morning.'

'I'll bring you some tea, just as soon as I've got this pie in the oven.'

'Thank you, Mrs Brindley. You're very kind.'

'I reckon you need a bit of kindness.' She paused. 'It's early days, I know, but have you made any decisions yet?'

The housekeeper's job was uncertain now and Nancy felt a duty to be as honest as she could, though her mind was a jumble and she was unsure of her first move.

'Only that I need to think about selling the house. But that will take weeks, and there'll be a new owner. I'll make sure to recommend you when the time comes.'

Mrs Brindley gave a small puff of air. 'I thought that was how it would be. Well, I can't blame you. Such a big place to keep going with only you to rattle around in it.'

Nancy gave a faint smile and walked back up the stairs to Leo's study. It wasn't the most sensitive phrase to describe her new widowhood, but the woman had meant it kindly. Sitting heavily down on the leather swivel chair that Leo had loved, she stared at the papers strewn across his desk. They had been abandoned when he'd been whisked into hospital and, though she'd offered to sort them, he'd insisted he'd do it himself. *I'll be back very soon*, he'd promised her.

Nancy felt her eyes mist and the lump, that was constantly in her throat, grow. Get a grip, she told herself. Leo had been dead for nearly two weeks and she must try to be practical. Flicking through the papers, she pulled out anything she could deal with immediately. One or two telephone calls to cancel magazine subscriptions, several bills to pay, a book to return to a colleague in Italy, but otherwise little else. Shuffling the remaining papers into a single pile, she put them aside for Dominic Gray. He would be the one to wind up Leo's business dealings.

Tidying the desk had soothed her. Stupidly, she felt that in some way she'd regained control over her life. And she did have control, she told herself. She was going back to work soon and she'd search for somewhere to live. Somewhere smaller and easier to take care of, where she wouldn't need a housekeeper or a gardener or anyone other than herself. Her first task then was to put the house up for sale. There was an estate agent in Paddington that she'd passed this morning on her way to the station with Perry. Should she try there?

'I'm just popping out to do some shopping.' Mrs Brindley had arrived with a tray of tea and biscuits. 'Stock up on the basics. Is there anything you need in particular?'

'I don't think so. I've a couple of calls to make, some letters to answer. Then I'll start looking for an estate agent.'

Mrs Brindley's face cracked into a rare smile. 'That one in Baker Street is good, so I've heard. Gentlemanly, you know.'

'I didn't even realise there was one in Baker Street, so thank you. Maybe I'll go tomorrow.'

Mrs Brindley nodded. 'Death's a painful business, but it's good to get on with things.'

It took a while after the housekeeper had left for Nancy to finish her telephone calls and settle into answering the many condolence letters she'd received from Leo's clients and colleagues. She was unsure if this was the correct protocol, but she needed to write for her own sake, to say a thank you for the kind thoughts they'd sent. She was halfway through the second letter when out of the blue a wave of grief swept over her, forcing her to put the pen down and search for a handkerchief. It seemed she could only manage one letter at a time. Death *was* a painful business.

She looked out of the window. It had begun to rain again, although in the freezing temperature it was turning to sleet. Hardly a day for venturing out, but she was desperate to be active. Desperate to feel fresh air on her face. Running up to her bedroom, she pulled from the wardrobe her raincoat and a pair of leather boots. Gloves and scarf were gathered up from the hall, along with Leo's large umbrella, that had been big enough to shelter the pair of them. Don't start thinking, she warned herself.

Baker Street was only minutes away and she easily found the estate agents that Mrs Brindley had mentioned. Soon she was thawing out in a warm office, with a Mr Pettigrew smiling benignly across the desk.

'So, Cavendish Street,' he said. 'A desirable address. Elegant houses, most elegant. I doubt we will have trouble in selling your home, Mrs Tremayne. I'll need to view, of course—to arrive at an appropriate price. I can call tomorrow if that would suit. It shouldn't take long, and then if you like our terms, I can send my assistant to measure. If all goes well, we could have the house advertised for sale within the week. What do you say?' He beamed expectantly at her.

'Yes… I suppose… it's quicker than I thought…' She was stuttering.

'You do wish to sell?'

'I must,' she said firmly. 'It's only that… my husband was buried two days ago and I'm still unused to my new situation.'

Mr Pettigrew bounced up from his chair and almost scampered around the desk. 'My dear lady, I am so sorry. How insensitive of me! But I had no idea. If you wish to delay, there is no problem. I will give you my card and you can telephone at any time to make an appointment.'

Nancy took the card and tried to steady herself. 'You're very understanding, and thank you. But I don't wish to delay, really I don't. There's no point. Please come tomorrow and look around. Say eleven o'clock?'

He beamed again. 'Perfect. If that is all...' When she nodded, he stood up and shook her hand. 'Allow me to escort you out.' With a flourish, he opened the glass door to the street. 'I will see you tomorrow, Mrs Tremayne.'

She stumbled out of the agent's office, her legs flimsy and barely able to support her. Is this what it was going to be like? She would make a decision, only to be plagued with uncertainty. She would ask people to do things for her, only to backtrack immediately. She needed that grip more than she'd imagined.

Battered by the shards of ice blowing in her face, she walked slowly back to Cavendish Street. Gradually, her breathing settled and her pulse quietened. She could do this, she told herself.

There was someone at her front door, standing at the top of the steps. A figure that wasn't Mrs Brindley's. Frowning, she quickened her pace. The figure turned at the sound of footsteps ringing in the thin air. Nancy came to an abrupt halt, her mouth half open. Her father! A father she hadn't seen for nearly four years. Drawing nearer, she noticed how much older Harry Nicholson looked, how much more rounded his shoulders. The lines on his face, too, were more deeply carved.

'Hello, Nancy,' he said, trying for a jovial tone that was too nervous to be successful.

'Hello,' was all she could manage. She couldn't bring herself to call him Dad. His right to be her father had ceased the moment he'd refused to save her from a man who was plainly unhinged.

'Did you want something from me?' she asked.

It was a stupid question. Naturally he wanted something or he wouldn't be here. Her stomach tightened into a hard knot. Had he brought Philip March with him? Was that why he was making this visit, to pressure her again into the marriage she'd abandoned years ago, now that she was a widow? Surely, not even her father could be that crass. Nevertheless, she looked nervously around, trying for a glimpse of anyone who might be loitering amid the plane trees that lined the street, or lurking down the basement steps of adjoining houses.

'It's all right,' Harry Nicholson said. 'Don't worry. I'm on my own. I want to talk to you, Nancy, that's all. Can we go in?'

Reluctantly, she found her key and ushered him into the hall. Her father's gaze took in the cream embossed walls, the Persian rugs, the several small sculptures.

'Quite a house you've got here.'

'You better come into the sitting room.'

She tried not to sound impatient, but she wanted her father gone before Mrs Brindley returned—explanations would be needed that she didn't want to offer. Leading the way into the high-ceilinged room, she took a seat in her favourite chair, while her father plumped himself down on the velvet-covered sofa.

'A bit of a difference from that place you had in Chilworth Road,' he said admiringly, his eyes continuing to wander. He seemed stunned by seeing his daughter in such beautiful surroundings. 'You did well, my girl.'

'What is it you want? she asked crisply.

'Want? I don't want anything and there's no need to take that tone, Nancy. I know we've had a few disagreements in the past, but we shouldn't let that spoil the future.'

His willingness to sweep away the horrors she endured, to label them as innocuous "disagreements", almost made Nancy show him the door, but she dug her fingernails into her hands and kept her lips tightly pressed.

Harry Nicholson leaned towards her. 'The thing is, my dear, you're a widow now.'

Nancy felt like screaming. Did he think she didn't know that?

'You're on your own in the world,' he went on. 'Granted, you've got this big house and no doubt your husband's left you well-placed, but it's not the same as having family, is it?'

'I don't have a family,' she said icily.

'That's nonsense.' His tone was belligerent. 'You have a family all right, and we're willing to let the past be the past, your mother and I. We'd like you to come home. Stay with us for a while.'

'In Riversley?' She was astonished.

'In Riversley, yes. Why? Isn't the bungalow grand enough for you now?'

She didn't answer the question, but instead asked one of her own. 'Why have you turned up now? You've known where I lived for the last two years. Philip March would have told you—after he'd travelled to Cornwall and failed to kill me.'

Her father's face blanched. 'What do you mean?'

'I think you know. Or can guess. The letter I sent to reassure you that I was well and happy, the letter you made sure to show Philip, allowed him to trace me. He ran me to ground in Cornwall, after Leo's father had suffered a massive heart attack, and followed me there with the sole intention of killing. And why? Because I'd dared to marry another man.'

For a long time, her father said nothing. 'I didn't know,' he mumbled at last. 'We didn't know. Philip did come by. Told us how you were married to some high-up bloke in art and living in a posh house in London, but then he disappeared.' Harry paused. 'He did seem strange.'

'He's not strange. He's insane.'

'I said to your mother, that man's changed. He's not what he was.'

Nancy jumped up from her chair, and walked to the French doors and back again, marking an agitated path across the deep pile of the carpet. 'He hasn't changed. Don't you understand still? He was always mad. He just managed to appear normal. It was a façade, buttering you up, smoothing your feathers. He was very good at that, but underneath he was, and is, a cess pit of anger and bitterness. He is a dangerous man and always has been.'

'But are you sure… about him wanting to hurt you?'

She stopped walking at the sofa and looked down at her father. 'Believe me, I'm sure.'

There was another long silence. Harry Nicholson began shaking his head. 'I don't know what to say.'

'Sorry might be a good start.'

'We believed… we believed…'

'Yes, you did. You preferred to believe Philip March rather than your own daughter. I'm not sure what lies behind your visit here or behind the invitation to Riversley, but I do know that I won't be coming home, as you call it. It isn't my home, it never was. Now, I'm sure you'll appreciate that I have a good many things to do. And you will be needing to catch a train back to Hampshire.'

She walked to the doorway, forcing her father to follow. On the front step, she gave him a brief nod and watched as he walked down the steps, his shoulders seeming to sag more heavily. Out of the corner of her eye, Nancy caught sight of Mrs Brindley turning the corner from the other end of the street. The housekeeper had her head down against the sleet and hadn't seen Nancy's visitor walking in the opposite direction. At least, no explanations would be needed.

Standing in the hall, Nancy's head thrummed and her chest felt stifled, as though her father had taken up the very air she breathed. It had been a horribly upsetting visit—for them both, she imagined—but why had he appeared out of the blue and why now?

# Chapter Five

Mrs Brindley had left for home and Nancy settled to eat a lonely meal at the kitchen table—she never bothered with the dining room now. She and Leo had eaten here all winter. It was cosier in the kitchen and easier to clear the dishes. Pushing her empty plate aside, she sat, elbows propped on the long wooden table, turning over in her mind how in these last few weeks since Leo became so ill, her feelings about the house had changed slightly. The bungalow in Riversley had never been home to her. She had always been a cuckoo in the nest, the longed-for child who'd turned out to be the wrong sex. Not the son they had wanted. Not the girl they had wanted either. A renegade who'd decided to live her own life and not theirs, leaving Hampshire for London at too young an age, but finding a job she loved at the auction house.

She'd never felt she belonged in Cavendish Street either. This was Leo's house, Leo's home, and she was here on sufferance, merely perching. Mrs Brindley had certainly treated her so, until this most difficult winter that they'd navigated together. But increasingly, Nancy no longer perched and the house had come to feel more and more like a sanctuary. Ironic, now that she was selling.

Penleven, though, was a different matter entirely. The

Cornish house would never feel welcoming, no matter how much she tried. Perry, bless him, had offered her a home there if she wanted. She'd said all the right things, but she would never take up the offer. It was fortunate her work would always be in London, saving her from having to fabricate excuses.

Taking her dishes to the sink, Nancy wondered how she was to fill the evening. She couldn't read, her mind wandered too much and was filled with images she'd rather forget. And it was too early to go to bed. There was a general knowledge quiz on the Light Programme, she remembered. The one with Franklin Engelman. She glanced up at the kitchen clock—the programme would have started by now—but it would fill half an hour.

She was tuning in the wireless when the doorbell rang. Her father again? Surely he would have caught a train back to Riversley by now. Who then? Archie? Could it be Archie?

She rushed up the stairs and into the hall, then stopped dead. What if it wasn't? Her father's visit had sharpened old fears and, wavering at the front door, her hand on the latch, she felt certain it was March on the other side. She'd known he would come eventually. He had a job to finish. As she stood there, the bell rang again, this time seeming more insistent. Nancy took a deep breath and slipped on the safety chain, opening the door no more than an inch. It was a man, glancing idly down the street, his back to her. Not her father. Not Archie. Not March either. The man turned.

'Sorry, Mrs Tremayne, I shouldn't call so late, but it's been a bit of a madhouse at Abingers today and I've only just got away. I left some stuff in Leo's office. Would it be okay to collect it?'

'Mr Gray.' She breathed out slowly, slipping back the

safety chain.

'Is everything all right?' he asked in a worried voice. 'You look positively spooked.'

'I'm sorry. I'm just a bit distracted.'

'My fault entirely. I would have left it to the morning, but I've another crazy day waiting for me tomorrow.

'Come in. You know your way to the office.'

He nodded and walked along the hall to the far door. Nancy retreated to the sitting room to wait for him, but he was gone only minutes and returned with a sheaf of papers in his hand, waving them at her from the doorway. 'Easy to find,' he said.

He glanced around the room, his gaze, Nancy saw, fastened on the brightly coloured cardigan she had pulled from Leo's bag when she'd brought it home from the hospital. It had been Archie's cardigan, knitted by his mother, but Leo had taken a fancy to it one winter when he was unwell and had worn it ever since. Gray seemed fixated by it. Did he think she had a man living with her?

'I suppose you wouldn't have a cup of tea on the go would you?' he asked suddenly.

'Yes, of course,' she stammered. 'How thoughtless of me. You've been working late. You must be hungry as well as thirsty.'

'I was going to get a sandwich at the pub round the corner, but they don't serve tea and I don't think I could cope with beer at the moment and still stand up.'

'Come down to the kitchen. I'm sure there must be something I can make into a sandwich.'

A chunk of bread, several slices of ham and a helping of pickle, along with a fresh pot of tea, had Dominic eating with enjoyment.

'Why are you so busy at Abingers?' she asked, taking a

stool opposite him.

'An exhibition. One of the specials. It's when… but you'll know. You worked there, didn't you, I think Leo told me?'

'I did. It's where we met. I remember arranging several of those special exhibitions. I know how much work they take to be successful.'

'I imagine these days you prefer art restoration.' He took a large gulp of tea.

'I love it,' Nancy said simply.

'And you'll be going back the studio?' It was a tentative question.

'There's no reason for me not to.'

Particularly as Leo is no longer here to complain, she thought. Complain at how many hours I'm working and how much more I should be at home. Irritated with herself, she pushed the thought aside. It was too disloyal.

'That was good.' Dominic wiped his mouth on the napkin she'd provided and emptied his teacup.

'And you, Mr Gray? Will you be going back to working full-time at Abingers?'

Leo's death did mean change for some—for Gray, for Mrs Brindley, for her.

'They've given me my old position back,' he confirmed. 'That was a relief. I didn't think you'd want to keep me on here and I was concerned I'd only have half a job.'

'There are some papers still on Leo's desk,' she said. 'Or are they the ones you've taken?'

He shook his head. 'These—' he pointed to the pile of papers sitting on the corner of the kitchen table—'were in the filing cabinet. They'll be useful for the leaflets I'm planning. I'm hoping to get a batch printed and sent out to clients once the exhibition has ended.' He paused for a moment. 'Look, why don't I come back another time and have a look at what's left?'

'If you wouldn't mind. There must be people to contact. Leo's diary has events he pencilled in months ago.'

'Don't worry, I'll sort it out. It shouldn't take long. You'll have the house to yourself very soon—unless you were thinking of selling, of course.'

'I am,' she said. 'And soon.'

Nancy didn't know why she had told him. He wasn't a friend or any kind of intimate. He'd been Leo's part-time assistant and she had hardly seen him during the months he'd worked for her husband. Hearing the front door open and shut was her only indication he'd even been in the house. But this evening, he'd rescued her from a sadness that was difficult to keep at bay. It had been good to sit and talk normally—without the tension of being with someone like Perry, who was suffering as badly as she, perhaps even more. Or someone like her father, she thought darkly, with all the dreadful baggage their relationship carried. Dominic Gray was smart and polite and good company.

'I'd better be getting off now,' he said, taking his empty dishes to the sink. 'Many thanks for the refreshments, Mrs Tremayne—it's set me up for the journey home.'

Nancy didn't ask where home was. In her present vulnerability, it was best not to make too much of a friend of someone she hardly knew.

She went to slide from her seat, but he held up his hand. 'Please, don't get up. I can let myself out. But if I could use your bathroom before I go…'

'Of course. On the first floor. Second door on the right.'

'Thanks. Let me know when I can come by and I'll sort the last of those papers.'

'You'll be too busy for a while, I imagine.'

'I could call in after work one day. Not as late as this, though.'

'I'm always here,' she said simply.

# *Chapter Six*

The previous spring when he'd left his job with Leo Tremayne, Archie had signed up with an employment agency that until now had failed to provide employment. He'd found work mainly through word of mouth—there were plenty of businesses in the East End needing help—and Archie's experience of keeping accounts, making sense of legal documents, not to mention running an efficient office, ensured he'd never been without a job, even though most were badly paid.

When the call came from Bloomsbury Clerical, he was surprised and not that thrilled. The funeral was still on his mind, the thought of Nancy always present, and he'd almost decided to catch a train back to Cornwall—clear his head perhaps, enjoy home, spend time with Ma. But the woman at the agency sounded excited, their new client evidently something of a catch for them. *Abingers,* she announced grandly, *it's one of the best auction houses in London.* Archie didn't know whether to laugh out loud or cry into his handkerchief. Life couldn't get more bizarre. Or painful.

He was needed at the firm to organise an office whose usual occupant had been sick for several months, his work having fallen into disarray. It was a Mr Harker that Archie would be working for, if he took the job. The woman's tone suggested he'd be mad to turn the opportunity down. Harker had been Nancy's former boss, Archie knew. It could be awkward following in her footsteps, but also strangely comforting. He'd put the Cornish trip on hold for a while, he decided.

His sister-in-law, Grace, rang that evening, using Ma's phone.

*Rich is fishin'*, she said. *No idea when he'll be 'ome, but Perran Tremayne came back today, a walkin' dollop of misery*. Penleven was a sad place, apparently, and Grace no longer enjoyed going there, but old man Tremayne needed help and it was a job after all. *The fishin' don't bring in much still and the Tremaynes pay well. So how's Nancy, poor maid? I wanted to telephone but then thought best not. Rich and I sent a card and some flowers.*

Archie was forced to confess that he'd caught only a glimpse of Nancy at the funeral and hadn't spoken to her since.

*What's wrong with you, Archie Jago?* Grace scolded.*The girl's just lost her 'usband and you aren't speaking to her? Shame on you.*

After that drubbing, he'd reconsidered. Was he being foolish in keeping away from Nancy, unkind even? Should he at least telephone her? She'd be busy, he told himself. There'd be a lot of stuff to sort out, the funeral was only the start of it. She'd sell the house in Cavendish Street almost certainly—it was the sensible thing to do—and she'd have a four storey house to pack up. That would take time and she wouldn't want him under her feet. Everything was just fine as it was, he managed to persuade himself.

He'd lose himself in work, that was the answer, but when next morning he walked through Abingers' revolving doors, he came close to changing his mind. A man wearing a suit he appeared to have been poured into, strode across the impressive foyer to meet him.

'Are you the agency wallah?' he asked, disdain sounding in every syllable.

'Bloomsbury Clerical told me you have a job you need doing.'

Archie made sure he sounded as disdainful. This was the same creepy bloke who'd had his hand on Nancy's arm at the funeral. The one Leo had taken on after he'd left. How ever had his boss got on with this idiot? And now that Leo had gone, was the man still hanging around Cavendish Street? Archie felt an instant hatred.

'Come with me.' The man's command was abrupt, but Archie stayed exactly where he was. Dominic Gray turned. 'Are you coming or not?'

'Probably not. If they're all tusses like you, I don't want to work here.'

Gray couldn't have understood "tuss", it was a particularly Cornish insult, but he'd understood the tone. A flash of anger lit the man's face, then he straightened his shoulders, pulled his jacket sleeves down, and said in a more conciliatory tone, 'Mr Harker is waiting for you. He's in need of your services.'

'Let's hope he's a bit more polite than you then.'

The man's lips closed tightly. 'Follow me, please,' he said, making sure to emphasise the "please".

*

Mr Pettigrew rang the front door bell at exactly eleven o'clock. His manner was kind but efficient, his tour of the entire house from basement kitchen to the top floor apartment that had once been Archie's home, was completed within twenty minutes. Nancy would liked to have offered him a cup of tea, but dared not intrude into the kitchen. Mrs Brindley was cooking and not in the best of moods. She'd barely acknowledged the agent when he'd looked in, making it plain she considered him a trespasser. Saying goodbye to Mr Pettigrew as soon as she politely could, became Nancy's main concern.

He was as swift in his calculations as he had been in viewing the house. A few scribbled numbers on the pad he carried, and he was ready.

'A lovely house, Mrs Tremayne,' he announced. 'We will have no trouble in selling it for you—and at an excellent price.' There was pride in his voice. 'What do you say to four thousand pounds?'

Nancy was so taken aback that she didn't answer straightaway. The house was large and part of a prestigious terrace of townhouses, but the sheer size of the figure the agent had quoted was astonishing.

'You don't consider it sufficient?' he enquired anxiously.

'No, no. Nothing like that. I'm surprised, that's all,' she said inadequately.

'I take it then that you are happy we go ahead?'

She nodded.

'I will send Mr Beecham around tomorrow. He's a pleasant young man and knows his job. Just leave him to measure and we'll have the draft details to you by the end of the week.'

'Thank you, Mr Pettigrew,' she said faintly, opening the front door for him. Still dazed, she watched as he skipped down the front steps.

Wandering back to the sitting room, she plumped herself down in one of the chairs. The price had taken her breath away. If she had that much money, she could easily buy the kind of small house she had in mind, and put away enough for the future.

For a while, she sat imagining the house she'd choose, the décor she'd have, the furnishings. Then she looked around the room she was sitting in and her heart gave a jolt. She would have to sell everything here, she realised. It was all too grand for a small house. The antique furniture Leo had collected over the years, the Persian rugs, the paintings, the rare ornaments.

She frowned. There had been something that bothered her, she remembered now, when she'd been escorting Mr Pettigrew around the house. Something that wasn't quite right. Had it been in the dining room? She so rarely went there these days that it was likely she'd notice anything unusual. Retracing her steps to the room, she glanced around and felt puzzled. The place was exactly as she'd seen it when she and Leo had last eaten there, long before Christmas. Long before Leo had developed the second bout of bronchitis.

Nancy turned in a circle, taking in the whole room, her gaze landing on the Regency sideboard. That was it! The Sevres porcelain bowl. The beautiful Bleu Royal pot pourri bowl and cover, a particular favourite of Leo's, but no longer where it should be. What had happened to it?

She walked down the stairs to the basement where Mrs Brindley was washing the tiled floor.

'The pot pourri bowl—in the dining room? Did you see it when you dusted last?'

'I haven't been in the room for a few days,' the housekeeper said, straightening up. 'When I last dusted, it was where it always is—on the cherrywood sideboard.'

'How strange. It's not there now.'

'You're sure it's missing?'

'Quite sure.' Nancy shook her head. 'Never mind, I expect it will turn up. Eventually.'

*

Mr Beecham arrived the next morning as promptly as his employer, and spent several meticulous hours measuring each room, the basement first on his list. Once he'd moved upstairs, Nancy retreated to the kitchen.

'Do you mind if I stay a while,' she asked the housekeeper, 'until Mr Beecham has left.'

Mrs Brindley waved Nancy to take a seat. 'I'm nearly finished here. I thought I'd go home a bit early today, if that's okay. With that man in and out of every room, cleaning is impossible.'

'That's fine. The house is spotless anyway, and I cleaned the bathroom myself this morning.'

She'd wanted to do it. Mrs Brindley would have packed Leo's belongings away—his toothbrush, his shaving brush and razor, the towel he'd last used. The housekeeper had been itching to do it for days. But while his things were still in the bathroom, Nancy could pretend to herself that he wasn't too far away.

'Can I help here?' she asked.

'I've finished the veg—you can take the peelings out to the dustbin if you've a mind. The weather's that cold, my arthritis is playing up.'

'Of course I will.' Nancy jumped down from the stool. 'Let me know what else I can do. I'm home for a while and I've plenty of time. Connie is happy that I don't go back to the studio just yet.'

'I should think so,' Mrs Brindley grumbled. 'You shouldn't rightly be going back for months.'

Nancy wrapped the vegetable peelings in several sheets of newspaper and walked out into the paved courtyard at the rear of the house. Mrs Brindley was right, it *was* freezing. She felt a twinge of guilt. The housekeeper had a complicated journey to get to Cavendish Street. Two buses, Mrs Brindley had told her once. Perhaps she should suggest a part-time arrangement for the rest of the winter, until the house was sold.

Pulling the lid from the dustbin, she was about to empty her newspaper bundle inside when her hand was arrested. Her eyes fixed on the contents of the bin. She was incredulous. It was Leo's bowl, the beautiful Sevres from the dining room, except that now it was in a hundred pieces.

Tenderly, she picked out some of the larger shards and lay them in her palm, feeling as though she would burst into tears. The object was so badly smashed there was no chance of ever repairing it. But how it had got here? And who had broken it?

She walked slowly back into the kitchen. 'I've found the bowl, Mrs Brindley.' She almost whispered the words. 'The pot pourri bowl.'

'You said it would turn up,' the housekeeper said complacently, running hot water into a washing- up bowl.

'But look at it.' Her voice was shaking now.

The woman turned, staring hard at what lay in Nancy's outstretched hands. 'Oh my!' she exclaimed.

'Have you any idea how it could have happened?'

Mrs Brindley glared at her. Yanking the teatowel from its rail, she gave her hands a vicious wipe. 'Are you suggesting I broke it?'

'No, of course not. I just wondered if...'

'Because if you are,' the woman continued, 'I think it's time for me to go.'

'Please don't. I'm not suggesting any such thing.'

'Still...' The housekeeper stood firm, hands on her hips. 'I've had an offer of a job nearer home. Just round the corner, in fact. Big house, nice family. Mebbe it's time for me to move. Makes sense—this house will be sold in a week or so. And at least you won't have anyone to blame for anything else that gets broken.' She untied her pinafore and bundled it into the straw shopping bag she always carried.

'I don't—' Nancy began, when Mr Beecham appeared in the kitchen doorway, having given a gentle knock.

'All done, Mrs Tremayne. Mr Pettigrew will be in touch.'

'Thank you,' she said distractedly. 'Let me see you out.'

She was closing the front door after the young man, when Mrs Brindley appeared at her side.

'I'm off now. You know my address, Mrs Tremayne. You can send any money that's owing.'

The housekeeper swept past and down the front steps before Nancy could say another word. Feeling utterly devastated, she closed the door behind her. How on earth had that happened? She had genuinely not been accusing the woman of breaking the bowl, though now she could see it might have sounded as though she were. But to walk out like that, after all these years... perhaps the housekeeper had been minded to leave anyway, at a moment she chose, and the broken bowl provided a good enough reason. Mrs Brindley had loved Leo and she had certainly never loved his wife. But Leo was no more, and now Nancy had been left completely alone.

# Chapter Seven

Archie had enjoyed his first few days at Abingers more than he'd expected. Mr Harker turned out to be an old-school disciplinarian, but he was fair and straightforward. He reminded Archie of one of the sergeants he'd had during his six years in the army. Harker was a man he could get on with. He lived in the adjoining office, not that Archie's work space could be termed an office. It was more like a cupboard, partitioned off the larger room next door. Abingers staff must have grown while the building hadn't.

Dominic Gray shared Harker's office, though he was rarely at his desk. It seemed he was required to run frequent errands by the Managing Director, and would reappear an hour or so later wearing a smug expression. Archie ignored him. He liked the work at the auction house better than any he'd had since leaving Leo, and he'd counselled himself not to let personal feelings get in the way of a comfortable berth.

He'd been busy this morning organising the catalogue for an upcoming sale. There was a huge amount of detail to research and collate. Occasionally the artist was unknown and an attribution was necessary or, in some cases, the mention of a studio or a circle to which the artist belonged. The style or manner of the painting needed inclusion, too, and whether it was signed or inscribed, and what date, if any, it bore. It was painstaking work, each item differently designated.

Feeling his legs stiff and his shoulders acquiring a permanent hunch, he decided on a short walk. A stroll and a quiet smoke would set him up for the rest of the morning. Harker had caught him at it once or twice, but Archie never took more than a few minutes, and so far he'd avoided a warning. Reaching the door of his room, he heard a voice from the office next door. Unusually, it was Gray's, and he was on the telephone.

'I'm doing my best,' the man protested. He sounded angry. 'I'm working on it, for Godsake. You've got to give me time. It's not something I can rush.'

There was a lull while Gray listened to whatever his caller had to say. 'Look, it's going well,' he insisted, when he could speak again. 'I'll have it in the bag in no time. Then you can move in.'

Becoming aware that Mr Harker had appeared at the end of the corridor, Archie melted back into his office but, as soon he could, he resumed his listening post. He'd thought Dominic Gray was shady and now he was certain. The bloke was up to something, he'd put his money on it.

'I'll have a look this evening, Mr Harker,' Gray was saying. 'I was planning to go round to Cavendish Street—there's still some papers Mrs Tremayne wanted me to sort through. Maybe the document you need is among those.'

'You don't think it's too soon to call?' Harker said. 'I wouldn't want Mrs Tremayne to feel we're intruding. The professor's funeral was only days ago and I've no wish to upset his widow.'

'It won't be a problem,' Gray said airily. 'I've already called at Cavendish Street.' There was a pause—was Harker looking askance, Archie wondered?—before Gray said, 'Mrs Tremayne was happy to see me and is keen to have her husband's desk cleared. I'll go after work today.'

Archie felt his breath constricted and his skin suddenly too tight. He wanted to break free, burst into the next office and take Gray by the throat. The man was a slimy toad, and Archie wanted him away from the house. Away from Nancy.

Harker's response was unintelligible, but Archie had heard enough. Abandoning the idea of a cigarette, he went back to his desk. Somehow he got through the rest of the day, but at five o'clock he was in the foyer of the building, waiting for Gray to leave. He hadn't long to idle. Hearing the man's voice as the lift doors opened, he turned to face the nearest wall, apparently engrossed in studying a painting of Abingers' founder.

As soon as Gray walked outside, Archie followed. He knew the way to Cavendish Street blindfolded, but he wanted to keep the man in sight, monitor the route he took. Why would Gray call on Nancy twice? Why not scoop up every piece of paper on his first visit and take all of it back to the auction house for Harker to see? Unless there was something else going on.

For a moment, Dominic Gray disappeared from sight and Archie's heart leapt at the thought that maybe he'd changed his mind. But then the man was coming out of one of the few off-licenses in the district, carrying a bottle of wine. It confirmed all Archie's fears. Why did he need wine to collect a handful of papers?

Turning the corner into Cavendish Street, Archie slowed his pace. It was already dark and the street lights gave little illumination. The trees on either side of the street were bare of leaves, but even so, they provided concealment. Watching, he saw Gray ring the doorbell of number twenty-two, heard a light voice, then saw him disappear.

Archie was torn, unsure of what he should do. Interrupt

this cosy tête a tête? Tackle Gray when he emerged and threaten him to keep away in the future? Or simply maintain a close watch on the man? If Gray was genuinely doing Harker's bidding, there should be no further need for him to call at the house, with or without wine.

*

Nancy had lain awake last night, troubled by the broken pot pourri bowl and Mrs Brindley's sudden departure. If the ornament had been there a few days ago—and the housekeeper was sure it had—how could it have been broken since? There had only been the two of them in the house to break it, except the agent and Mr Beecham. Could either of them be responsible? But she'd been with Mr Pettigrew the whole time he was in the house and the idea was ridiculous anyway. As for his assistant, it was possible, she supposed. He'd had the run of the place while she'd kept out of the way, but to get to the courtyard he would have had to use the rear door and she would surely have seen him walk past from where she was sitting in the kitchen.

There was something even more troubling. The bowl had been smashed into pieces. Very small pieces. It wasn't how an item of porcelain would look if it had been dropped accidentally. It was how it would look if a hammer had been deliberately wielded.

After that sleepless night, Nancy had felt drained and depressed, Leo's death hanging heavy in her heart. She'd needed to get out of the house, to feel herself making at least tentative steps forward. Dressing in her thickest coat and fur-lined boots, she'd taken the bus to the boroughs north of Marylebone, having decided to register with as many estate agents as she could find. North London was where her new home would be—Hampstead, Highgate, somewhere airy, more spacious, with plenty of green to please the eye. It would mean a longer journey to the studio, but she thought the compromise worth it.

Most of the day had been spent leaving her details with a number of agents, and being plied with leaflets, extolling the virtues of their various properties, none of which had immediate appeal. By the time she opened her own front door, dusk had fallen and she was numb with cold. Hot tea, that was the answer. Hanging up her coat on the bentwood stand, she ran down the stairs to the kitchen and had just put the kettle to boil when the doorbell rang.

She wasn't entirely delighted to see Dominic Gray on her doorstep. He was a nice enough man, but she'd been picturing the moment when she'd put her feet up on the sofa and enjoy a hot drink.

He waved a bottle of wine at her. 'A small present, Mrs Tremayne. For allowing me to disturb you again.'

Nancy was a little ashamed of how unwelcoming she felt. Pinning a smile on her face, she tried to sound enthusiastic. 'It's very nice to see you again, Mr Gray. Do come in. You'll find Leo's desk exactly as you left it. I haven't touched a thing since your last visit.'

He took care to scrape his boots on the front doormat and she was grateful for his thoughtfulness. It was a large house to keep pristine entirely on her own.

'May I offer you a cup of tea?'

'Not just now, thank you. I'd better get on with the job. Perhaps a glass of wine for you, though? Forgive me, but you look all-in. A glass of Beaujolais could be just the thing.'

Not the best idea, Nancy thought to herself. It was only just past six in the evening and she'd had nothing to eat for hours. Leo had been abstemious, only buying wine for the house if they were entertaining, and she was unused to drinking much.

'You might treat yourself?' Gray suggested, when he saw her hesitation. 'I'll get on in any case.'

Nancy took the bottle down to the kitchen where, in her absence, the kettle had adopted screech mode. Switching off the gas, she sank down on a stool. Perhaps Dominic was right. Perhaps a glass of wine would perk her up. She certainly needed it.

The Beaujolais was very good. She was no connoisseur, but the way it trickled down her throat—gently, slowly, warmly—had her fingers unfreeze and her feet thaw. Leaning against the kitchen table, she relaxed into a comfortable doze. It was a creak of the old walls settling into their night time slumber that had her look up at the kitchen clock. Dominic Gray was taking his time, she thought. Half an hour and counting.

At that moment, though, he came into the kitchen. 'All done. The desk is clear. Sorry I've been a while, but I took the liberty of looking through every drawer—just in case there were papers that we need at Abingers. Mr Harker's been chasing one particular document and seems convinced that Leo took it with him after the last exhibition.'

'Did you find it?' she asked anxiously.

'I'm not sure, but I've bundled everything I think might be useful into my briefcase and Harker can go through it all tomorrow.'

'Mr Harker is your boss?'

'In a way, though I answer mainly to Mr Simmonds. But, of course, you'll know them both.'

'Mr Harker trained me,' she said, sipping the last of her wine. 'Thank you for this.' She pointed to the bottle. 'It was an inspired choice. I am now thoroughly warm after a day tramping the icy streets of North London. But you should have a glass, too.'

'Thank you. I will, if that's okay. Just the one before I make the long journey home.'

He settled himself on a stool opposite. 'So how did you find Mr Harker? I won't tell, honestly.'

She laughed. 'There's nothing to tell. He was a very good boss—strict but fair and very knowledgeable.'

'I've found that, too, though I'm not sure our newest recruit thinks so.'

'You have new staff?'

'A temporary chap. He worked for your husband, I believe. I can't imagine how the two of them ever got on.'

'Archie?' Her voice wavered a little and she hoped he hadn't noticed.

'Archie Jago, that's the man. Surly chap, but perhaps Leo saw qualities in him that I don't.'

'Leo and Archie come from the same village in Cornwall. They were in the army together.'

She wanted to add that Archie had saved her husband's life, and hers, but she bit back the comment.

'Ah, a cosy arrangement.'

'Not really.' She felt annoyed, and probably sounded it. Archie was extremely good at his job and Leo had depended on him.

Gray backtracked. 'He seems pretty efficient, I grant you. I probably got on his wrong side.'

'It wouldn't be difficult. Archie can be prickly.'

'That smells delicious, whatever it is,' he said, changing the subject.

'I'd forgotten! It's a casserole Mrs Brindley made yesterday. I put the timer on before I left this morning.'

'How very civilised. But I mustn't stop you from eating.' With a smile, he got up from his stool.

'Why don't you stay and have some. Mrs Brindley is a very good cook.'

Nancy wasn't sure what had prompted her to make the offer, though it probably wasn't difficult to guess. It had been a cold, tiring day. She was alone in this large house and Dominic Gray was a friendly face. She missed Leo and she missed Archie—so very much.

'That's so kind of you.' Dominic jumped at the chance. 'Otherwise, I'll be going back to an icy flat and a plate of cold ham.'

'Good. Are you happy to eat here? The dining room can be a bit forbidding.'

Forbidding, and a room she no longer wanted to visit, not after the Sevres had been so comprehensively shattered.

'You have a very cosy kitchen. I'd love to eat here.'

The beef casserole was excellent, made even more so by several glasses of wine. They chatted continuously, Dominic an easy person to talk to, and it was only when Nancy put down her knife and fork, and went to take a last sip of wine, that she realised her glass was empty. She fixed the bottle with a slightly unfocussed eye. Had they really drunk that much? Had *she* drunk that much? It was so unlike her.

Gray slipped from his stool and collected their empty plates. 'I'll wash up. No, I insist.' He held up his hand as she began to protest. 'That was probably the best meal I've eaten for months. Washing a few dishes is a small price to pay. '

She smiled at him. He was a pleasant man and she was glad she'd invited him to stay. Putting the kettle to boil once more and setting out cups and saucers, she recounted her day's hunt for a new house.

'So you're going ahead with the sale?'

'This house is far too big for me. I need something a good deal smaller.'

'I can understand, though it does seem a shame to be selling such a lovely home. Have you ever thought of letting a part of it? Your husband's old assistant, Jago, had a flat here, didn't he? You could always let that. He might even like to come back himself.'

She frowned and he said quickly, 'Just a suggestion. I heard the chap tell Mr Harker that he had a long journey from wherever he lives.'

'I won't be letting any of the house,' she said firmly. 'Apart from anything else, I need a new beginning.'

'Of course,' he agreed. 'Hampstead, you say? It's a nice place. Villagey. Homely.'

'Perhaps that's why I'm attracted to it. The village aspect, I mean.'

'You don't come from London then?' He emptied the soapy water down the sink and dried his hands on the hanging towel.

'I was brought up in Riversley. It's a village in Hampshire, but I left at seventeen, and I've lived in London ever since.'

'That was a bold move. Coming to London at such a young age. But it obviously paid off.' She saw his eyes rove around the spacious kitchen. Is that what he thought, that she had come to London to snare a wealthy man?

'I guess it must have been hard at first, finding a job, finding somewhere to live.' His smile disarmed her.

'It was,' she said briefly, handing him a cup of tea.

'I'll drink this and then I'll be off. I wonder… you've been so kind, I'd like to repay your hospitality. How about lunch one day? I know a nice restaurant not far from Abingers—they've a decent menu.'

Nancy was going to refuse. Lunching with a single man would not meet with social approval, not so soon after her husband's death. But society was so often wrong about women's lives. A lunchtime appointment with a charming young man was innocent enough, and escaping these four walls could only be beneficial.

She took a sip of her tea. 'I'd love to come,' she said. 'Thank you.'

# *Chapter Eight*

The wine had given Nancy a headache she couldn't shift, and it was with bleary eyes the next morning that she peered out of the kitchen window at the frosty day beyond. The footsteps of passers-by—their feet and legs all she could see from the basement—rang tinnily in the freezing air.

Breakfast was a meal she couldn't face, settling instead for a shopping trip to replenish the larder. Grabbing the basket that Mrs Brindley always refused to use—*I have my own shopping bag which does me fine*—she donned the coat and boots abandoned from yesterday, and walked out into what was still only half-light.

The intense cold was a shock, but the air felt bracing and, by the time she reached the nearby parade of shops, she was feeling a good deal better. Mr Pettigrew had delivered draft details of the house when she was still asleep—the man was certainly efficient—and she'd managed a quick glance through them before she'd left the house. Her brain was still befuddled, but the leaflet appeared accurate and well-presented. Her shopping done, she resolved to walk on to Baker Street. She would call at the agency and confirm she was happy for the sale to go ahead.

'Your house will be in our window tomorrow morning—in pride of place,' Mr Pettigrew said, when she told him.

Leaping from his chair, he shook her hand so vigorously she feared her gloves might come adrift at the seams.

The die was cast and she was on the move. Bolstered by the thought, Nancy walked home with her mind full of plans, her first consideration how best to marshall the contents of the house. Her bedroom was where she'd begin, she decided, and as soon as she'd hung her coat and hat, she took the stairs to the first floor. From now on, there would be no more delay.

Her chest of drawers was the first to be cleared, then the tall oak wardrobe. Both were easy enough. Her collection of clothes was modest, a few light frocks from her stay in the Caribbean, one or two smart wool dresses, but mostly warm jumpers and skirts, the kind of thing she wore to the studio every day. From the back of the cupboard, she pulled out the pair of pedal pushers she'd taken to Rio and smiled at them. They had been quite daring at the time and Leo had laughed at her. Rio was where she had realised for the first time how ill he was, how unlikely to live to a great old age.

She sat down heavily on the bed, her body filled with sadness. They had had a difficult relationship, her desire to be independent, to act as her own person, clashing constantly with Leo's need to control his world. But they'd also had good times. Not just the trips to Venice and the Caribbean and the holiday they'd taken in Italy. But the evenings spent together, talking over their individual days, talking art most often. Now those same evening hours dragged, the wireless her only companion.

But this wasn't going to get the house sorted and packed, was it? She jumped up—it was time to move on to Leo's wardrobe, a chore she was dreading. Sorrow lay beyond its wooden doors and the mass of clothes a challenge. Leo had been asked to attend so many grand occasions that really he should have had two wardrobes all to himself.

A challenge for sure, but not in the way Nancy had expected. Opening the wardrobe doors wide, she was forced back, staggering as a myriad of small creatures flew at her face. There was an angry buzzing in her ears, in her hair, her raised arms soon red with stings as she tried to protect her face. Bees? Were they bees, she thought wildly? Then for a second, her vision cleared. Wasps!

She hesitated no longer. Slamming the wardrobe closed, she ran from the room and shut the door fast behind her. Her face and arms were burning with pain and she was barely able to make it to the kitchen and pull from a top cupboard the first aid box. Scrabbling through its contents, her body on fire, she searched desperately for a lotion to soothe the stings. Half the bottle had disappeared before she felt any relief, yet all the time her mind was spinning. How could that have happened? How could there be a wasps' nest in Leo's wardrobe? True, neither of them had opened its doors for several weeks, but a nest? It was impossible.

She groped her way to a stool. Impossible, unless…

It was happening again. The beaten man Archie had sent scurrying was back. She'd known, as soon as soon as she'd seen that wreath, it would be so. Archie had warned him never to come near Nancy again, but March was so possssive, so insanely jealous, that the words would have meant nothing. Not to a man prepared to kill. The broken bowl, the wasps. From the depths of her being, Nancy knew. March was back.

She couldn't prevent a small sob. She was alone now. No Leo to protect her. No Archie to rescue her. Not even Mrs Brindley to stand guard. But how had March got into the house? It wasn't worth speculating, she thought wearily. He would have found a way. He'd infiltrated Penleven without a problem.

She had never felt more isolated. But Rose. Could she

telephone Rose—this evening perhaps, when the children had gone to bed? She'd not spoken to her friend since the funeral. Rose had her hands full—a husband, a new job and two young children—but she wouldn't mind Nancy calling to chat. She'd mention what was happening in passing, not make a big thing of it, but ask Rose what she would do.

Meanwhile, Nancy had wasps trapped in her bedroom and she needed to make a call to the council. The pest control department would get rid of the insects. She didn't want to know how, she just wanted them away.

*

The council team had come and gone, leaving a strong smell of chemicals behind.

'I wouldn't sleep in that room tonight, Mrs Tremayne,' the lead man had warned her. 'The stuff we use is pretty bad for the lungs.'

Nancy was happy enough to sleep elsewhere. Along with the dining room, her bedroom felt now a place to avoid, but in any case, she was unlikely to sleep much tonight, or any night. The attack had been characteristic of March—it was how he operated. Once again, he was setting out to destroy her peace of mind, to cause her constant unease, so that she was always looking over her shoulder waiting for the next disaster. Before he ventured his final move, he would make her feel unsafe in her own home, unsafe in her own skin.

After a brief supper, she dialled Rose's number.

'How lovely to hear your voice, Nancy,' her friend said warmly. 'How are you, my love? Stupid question, I suppose.'

'I'm all right.' Nancy paused. 'Well, not really. Is it convenient to talk?'

'Couldn't be better. The terrors are in bed and Mike is watching our new television. I can't get him away from it!'

'Rose,' she said, 'I have a problem.'

Rose was quiet. She must be thinking that losing one's husband was problem enough.

'Apart from Leo, I mean,' Nancy continued. 'There have been incidents lately. Things that have unnerved me, and I don't know what best to do.'

'Tell me,' Rose invited.

Nancy hadn't meant to be so frank but, hearing her friend's voice again, she was unable to resist pouring out her fears. Her friend had warned her all those years ago that Philip March was not a good man, but she hadn't listened then. She was listening now.

'That is just awful,' Rose said, at the end of Nancy's recital. 'The man needs locking up.'

'I believed he'd gone for good,' she said miserably. 'In Cornwall. He followed me down there and tried to—'

'He followed you to Cornwall? How did he know where you were? Who you'd married?'

'It's a long story, but he tracked me down.'

'And…'

'He tried to kill me, Rose.'

There was a sharp intake of breath at the other end of the line. Nancy hadn't meant to sound so dramatic but, after all, it was the truth.

'My God, Nancy, why didn't you tell the police?'

'Because it would have involved Leo and he was so sure that by marrying me, he'd made me safe. The police wouldn't have believed me anyway. I've never involved them, not once since Philip's harassment started. He was a respectable journalist then, and I was a silly girl prone to hysterics. That's how he would have told it. Then I married Leo and it seemed fine. I never heard a thing from him. Never heard *of* him. Until Cornwall.'

'Well, he didn't kill you,' Rose said practically, 'so what happened?'

'Archie Jago turned up when I needed him most. He knocked Philip down and gave him his marching orders. He thought—and I hoped—that March wouldn't be a problem after that.'

'But he's come back.'

'He knows Leo has died. There was a wreath at the church—I recognised his writing. I wanted to tear it to pieces. My being a widow has given him a whole new opportunity. He's ready to attack again.'

'There must be someone you can ask for help.' Rose sounded despairing.

Nancy shook her head at the telephone. 'I'm selling the house. When it's gone, I can disappear, but it could be weeks before I can move. I don't know what to do.' There was anguish in her voice.

'Tell Archie,' Rose said unexpectedly. 'He helped you last time. And as soon as you can, get on a train to Dorset.'

'I'm not in touch with him,' she mumbled. 'And it wouldn't be fair to involve him again, not after… ' she trailed off.

'I don't know what's gone on between you both. I can only read through the lines in your letters, but you need to talk to him. At least, tell him what's been happening.'

It seemed so easy when Rose said it, but Nancy knew differently. It would be far from easy.

## Chapter Nine

The call over, Nancy sat deep in thought. Rose was right. Archie was the only person she could turn to, but how fair was that? After their trip to Rio, he'd walked away from a job he loved, to free himself, to free her, from a situation that was ruining their lives. Was it any different now, with Leo dead? In some ways, it seemed to Nancy even worse. Bad enough to betray a man who could fight back, but a man in his grave…a man you'd already wronged.

She felt confused, unsure. Would it really be another betrayal? Could she go to Archie as an ally who'd helped her in the past, without thought of what they'd once been to each other? Maybe. They were distant friends now, she told herself, even distant acquaintances. And if she didn't ask for help and March hurt her badly, how would Archie feel?

The East End was a large area and she had no idea if he still lived at the address she'd found on Leo's desk. He could well have moved after resigning from the job, somewhere cheaper perhaps, and it was unlikely that anyone in Reardon Road would know where he'd gone. She could always walk to Abingers, she supposed, and wait for Archie to emerge at the end of the working day, but she knew too many people there. How would she explain her presence and how cope with the inevitable questions of how she was feeling? At the funeral, she'd escaped with a few murmured words of thanks, but now she'd be expected to put on a brave façade and talk of Leo without breaking down. His death still felt too raw to do that. In particular, she'd find it awkward if she were to meet Dominic Gray there. He had telephoned only that afternoon, while the pest control people had been in the house, wanting to arrange their lunch.

How best to find Archie then? The card! The thought sprang fresh into her mind. The florist's card she had hidden in her handbag. She ran up the stairs to a bedroom that still smelt of powerful insecticide. The wasps might have been banished, but her skin continued to smart badly, and it would be a while before she forgot their attack.

The handbag she'd used on the day of the funeral was in the back of her cupboard—she still hadn't tackled Leo's wardrobe—and rummaging in its depths, she drew out the card. No address for Archie, of course, but it did have the telephone number of the florist where he had bought the wreath. She would make a call.

'I wonder if you can help me,' she began, hoping she might enlist her listener's sympathy. 'You made a wreath for my husband's funeral about two weeks ago and I'm keen to thank the sender. A Mr Archie Jago, but I don't know Mr Jago's address.'

'We don't usually give out customers' details,' the woman said cautiously.

'I do understand, but there were a lot of wreaths that day and I've managed to thank everyone else.' It was a white lie, but if it worked… She steadied herself to tell another. 'I'm not feeling my best at the moment, and it would help me to know I've done everything my husband would have wished.'

There was a pause while the florist thought about it, then a rustling of pages being turned.

'Two weeks ago, you say?'

'That's right. Jago is the name.'

'Yes, here it is. Ninety-eight Reardon Road, Stepney.'

'Thank you so much. I'll write to Mr Jago today.' Nancy replaced the receiver, feeling a tiny sense of satisfaction.

*

During that weekend, though, she became increasingly hesitant. Did she really have the right to intrude in Archie's life again? It was a question that circled endlessly in her mind and one to which she had no firm answer. Waking on Monday morning, she was still far from sure. She wondered what Leo would advise—he'd want her safe from March certainly—and, on the spur of the moment, she decided to visit the churchyard, buying a large bunch of daffodils on the way. She hadn't meant to return to his grave so soon, not until she'd reached some kind of equilibrium, but the need to be close to him was strong.

The churchyard emanated peace, and she decided to stay longer than she'd planned. Taking a seat on one of the wooden benches, she ate the sandwich she'd brought with her, then gathered her courage and walked towards the shining black gravestone that she'd chosen, it seemed now, an age ago. The wreaths had gone, she was glad to see, and she filled the metal vase with water from a nearby tap and arranged the flowers she'd brought.

She'd hope to sense Leo here, somehow to tune into his spirit and feel his protection once more, but there was nothing but a gravestone and a bunch of daffodils, their bright yellow heads moving in the breeze. As the light waned, and a dank mist began to rise from the ground, she made her decision. She would go, treating herself to a taxi all the way to Reardon Road and arriving at number ninety-eight just before five that evening.

Waiting outside the house in the dark and the cold, she was glad she'd chosen a nondescript coat and hat unlikely to draw anyone's attention. The house itself had seen better days, she thought, glancing up at its flaking paint and crumbling mortar. The entire terrace had seen better days, and was a far cry from Archie's neat apartment in Cavendish Street. What he'd given up for her!

It was nearly six before he arrived. He was fitting his key into the front door lock when she emerged from the shadows, her limbs stiff with cold.

'Archie.'

Her voice had him spin around.

'I'm sorry to come calling like this.' Why couldn't she keep the tremble from her voice? 'But I need to talk to you. I'm in trouble.'

He took the key from the lock and walked up to her. Beneath the light of the gas lamp—there were still gas lamps in the street—he looked older, more worn than when she'd said a last goodbye.

'What trouble?'

'Philip March is back.'

Archie swore under his breath and she saw his mouth tighten. 'Are you sure?'

'Have I ever been wrong about him? He—'

'We can't talk here. It's freezing. Charlie's caff is round the corner. It's near closing time, but he'll give us a cup of tea.'

It was a few minutes' walk only and the workmen's café was almost empty. Once they were settled at a table, Nancy grateful for the room's steamy warmth, she related the tale of the broken bowl and the horde of wasps. 'He knows Leo is dead,' she finished. 'He sent a wreath to the church, and now he's moving in for the—' She stopped mid-sentence, unable to finish.

'I had to tell someone,' she murmured, breathing in the familiar scent of pine soap, longing to reach out and pull his hands into hers. 'Rose said I should tell you.'

Archie sat looking at her for what seemed an age. 'What do you want me to do?' he asked at last. 'Short of taking up lodgings in Cavendish Street again, I can't see what help I can be. And I'm not going to do that, am I? In any case, there are others you can tell.'

'Like who? Mrs Brindley has left—she thought I was accusing her of breaking the Sevres bowl and walked out.'

'In a huff? She would. I didn't mean Mrs B. What about Dominic Gray?'

'How do you... of course, you're working at Abinger's now.'

'Right next door to the man himself. I hear he's been in the habit of calling on you.'

'He came for Leo's papers, that's all,' she said defensively.

'Really?'

'He's a pleasant man, Archie. He wants to be friendly.'

'There's your answer. Confide in him. Make him your knight in shining armour.' There was a bitter edge to Archie's voice.

'You're being ridiculous. Dominic Gray isn't a friend like—'

'Like me? But then I never was a friend, was I?'

Nancy felt deeply upset. There was anger in her, too. She'd depended on Archie through every trial she'd been through. Depended on him to be by her side. Now she faced danger again, perhaps the worst she ever had, he was forcing a quarrel on her. Was it jealousy or simply a wish to have nothing to do with her?

'Dominic Gray is a decent man,' she said defiantly.

Archie shook his head. 'He's a no-good.'

'How can you say that? You hardly know him. Is it because you're jealous?'

She spoke her thought aloud and now she was the one sounding ridiculous. Archie's mouth twisted, but he made no response. Infuriated, she burst out. 'I'll do as you advise. I'll tell Dominic. I'm having lunch with him.'

Archie shrugged his shoulders and pushed back his chair. 'Problem solved.' He was as hard as a piece of Cornish granite, Nancy thought. Giving nothing, feeling nothing. 'While you're at it, you could ask the delightful Dominic to move in with you. What better protection could you have? Right now, though, you'd better drink up. Charlie's hovering. He needs to close.'

Nancy couldn't speak, but picked up her handbag and walked to the door, thanking Charlie on the way out. 'I'm sorry I came,' she managed to say, once they were outside. 'I'm sorry I bothered you.'

She went to walk away, her heart so painful it felt as though cut in two, but at the last minute Archie reached out for her arm and pulled her close. 'Get rid of Gray,' he said urgently.

*

Archie walked back to his flat, unable to see straight for the red mist clouding his vision. He was angry—at Nancy for being so naïve about a snake such as Gray, but angry at himself that he'd sent her away hurt and bruised. He hadn't meant to. She'd caught him by surprise, arriving from nowhere, when she was the last person he'd expected to see.

What did she want from him? To be her shield in a battle with March? For that, he'd need to be far more than the acquaintance he'd turned into. It just wasn't on. Their relationship had run its course—it had never really stood a chance. Nancy's marriage had been imperfect, but she was loyal to the man who'd rescued her. Only once had she crossed the line and they'd never spoken of it again. It had been too precious, suggesting the future they could have had together, a future so badly desired, it was painful even now to think about.

She was having lunch with Gray, and she was right, he *was* jealous, and his jealousy had led him to condemn the man. It was possible that Gray might mean nothing but good in his dealings with Nancy, but Archie was pretty sure he was a man she should never trust. He hadn't forgotten the telephone call he'd overheard. Gray was plotting something with someone. It was all very vague, but he didn't want her mixed up in it.

He let himself into his flat and slumped on the bed, his appetite for supper vanished. Bloody Philip March! Why couldn't he leave the woman alone? The bloke was completely nuts, someone who needed locking away, never to see daylight again.

Perhaps the bowl and the wasps were all he'd attempt, Archie thought more hopefully. They could have been a warning, but nothing more. A reminder to Nancy that March hadn't forgotten her supposed misdeeds. Okay, the man knew Leo was dead, but did he know she was alone in the house? If he thought Leo's assistant was still living there, he might rein in his lunatic activities.

Archie laid back on the bed, his hands behind his head, gloom spreading slowly. It was unlikely that March didn't know the true score. He appeared to know a great deal about Cavendish Street, had managed to enter the house unseen, smash a bowl and plant a swarm of dangerous wasps, without leaving a trace.

Maybe he should hang around the house himself, Archie

thought, whenever he was free. Not so that Nancy would see him. Or Dominic Gray for that matter, but as a warning to March. If the bloke were keeping watch on Nancy—and Archie knew from Cornwall he was adept at spying—he'd winkle him out. Wait for a lonely moment perhaps and give him something to remember, something to send him packing for good.

## *Chapter Ten*

When Nancy woke the next morning to a clear blue sky, she determined to put last night's painful encounter behind her, and make this day a happy one. She would pay a visit to the studio. Spending an hour with her colleagues would be therapeutic and Connie, she knew, would be more than pleased to see her.

The business was a fair walking distance from Cavendish Street, tucked away among the Victorian terraces of Maida Vale and, despite the unbroken sunshine, Nancy was glad of a warm topcoat and fur-lined boots. In the crystalline air, the smell of paint and solvents hit her as she walked down the steps to the large basement space the studio occupied.

Two of her colleagues were at their easels, while Connie was using the spectrophotometer. Nancy had always loved the machine, loved the magic of its revelations: not only the particulars of an artist's chosen palette but often when and where he or she had painted the canvas, information that might otherwise remain unknown. The studio possessed an ex-ray machine for initial analysis, but it was the spectrophotometer that uncovered details of pigments indistinguishable to the human eye.

'Nancy! How good to see you!' Connie looked up from the machine she was operating.

'And to see you. All of you,' Nancy said, giving her colleagues a wave.

Connie resumed her gaze. 'You know, I could have sworn this blue was wholly ultramarine, but it turns out it's mainly azurite and much less expensive. The ultramarine has been used far more sparingly than I believed.'

'May I have a look?'

Connie made way for her. 'It's not easy to tell, is it?' Nancy murmured. 'But like you say, azurite seems predominant. I'm guessing the painting comes from the United States, or maybe Mexico.'

'My guess would be Mexico. I'm finished for the moment. Fancy a cup of coffee?'

It took only a few minutes for Connie to bring two steaming mugs to the workbench where Nancy had found a seat. 'Instant, I'm afraid,' she said, offering one of the mugs. 'Not a great taste, but better than Camp.'

'I don't mind what it is.' Nancy relaxed against the bench, absorbing the familiar smells, the sounds, the very texture of the studio. 'I can't wait to be back here.'

Connie was slow in responding. 'Are you sure about that?' Her brow puckered slightly. 'I don't know, of course,' she said, choosing her words carefully, 'but I wouldn't think that financially you will need to work.'

'I've not looked in detail at… it's still quite difficult.' Her voice faltered. 'But I'm sure I won't need to work. I never have, really. Not for financial reasons.' Leo's solicitor had written a few days ago to say that since all her husband's assets had been held jointly, probate was not involved and everything—house, furniture, money—had passed directly to her. 'It's just that I do.'

Connie's eyes held sympathy. 'I understand. And I'm glad. I wasn't looking forward to losing a valued colleague.'

'Not after all that mentoring you did,' Nancy joked. 'And now that I'm... that I'm on my own, I can return to the job full-time.'

Her friend leaned over and stroked the back of Nancy's hand. 'It might be best,' she suggested, 'if you continue with fewer hours. For a short while at least. You've had a rough time, Nancy. Not just losing your husband, but all the months that went before. Long, harrowing months. You must be tired out, though you might not realise the extent. Come back for a few days a week to start with, then see what you think.'

Nancy was disappointed. She had been longing to immerse herself in a world she loved, a world in which she felt secure, but Connie could be right.

'I suppose it makes sense,' she said. 'I'll be moving very soon and it's bound to take up a fair amount of time.'

'You've sold the house?'

'Not quite. Nothing has been signed yet, though there was a hint from the agent that he had a client in mind.'

'Have you decided where you'll move?'

'Hampstead,' she announced. 'I'm almost certain it will be Hampstead.'

'A good choice.' Connie collected up their empty mugs. 'A bit far out, but all that fresh air! You'll have to get a dog.'

She laughed. 'I can enjoy walking without a dog. There's not an enormous amount for sale there, but I've started getting leaflets through the post from various agents.'

'And?'

'There's one particular cottage I've rather fallen for. In Flask Lane. It's about the right size and it looks beautiful. Cream stucco with a balcony and roses around the front door.'

'I can see you there already! Have you actually viewed it?'

'I've made an appointment for the day after tomorrow. I thought I'd fit it in before you had me back on the treadmill.'

'Good luck with the viewing. You must let me know how it goes.'

Nancy took that as her signal to leave. Connie was a busy woman and she had already stayed too long chatting.

Feeling the need for more exercise, she let the bus pass her by, and set off on foot once more back to Cavendish Street. If her body was on the move and her eyes and mind busy with new scenes, she didn't have to think too deeply. About Leo. About Archie. About Philip March.

She had let herself into the hall before she realised that Mr Pettigrew was in the house. She'd entrusted him with a key and shouldn't have been surprised.

'So sorry, Mrs Tremayne.' He came bustling up to her. 'I did telephone to ask if it was convenient to call, but there was no reply.'

'I've been out,' she said simply. 'Are you showing someone around?'

'A charming gentleman. He has just sold his own house and was most keen to see yours. I have warned him that I have another interested buyer, but he was adamant he could top any offer that was made. Cavendish Street is where he wants to live.'

'And your other interested buyer? Is that definite?'

'Several people have expressed a strong interest, but one in particular—the gentleman is a banker—is extremely keen. He is moving back to this country from New York. He'll be based in the City but he knows Marylebone well, he's lived here before, and is keen to find a house in the district. He was most taken with the leaflet I posted him. His wife, too. Sometimes that is the most important factor. And he's able to pay cash. Always the best option, Mrs Tremayne. It would be a splendid sale.'

'Then let's hope it goes ahead. What about this morning's

client?' There had so far been no sign of the last minute visitor.

Mr Pettigrew allowed himself a smile. 'He is upstairs. I didn't think you would object to his wandering a little. I've taken him around the house, but he wanted to look again, by himself. People do. It's more relaxing that way. It can often lead to a sale you didn't think you would get.'

'Very relaxing, Mr Pettigrew,' a male voice said from the stairway, a pair of legs gradually coming into view.

Nancy stared aghast at the figure coming towards her.

The man held out his hand. 'My name is March,' he said. 'Philip March. How do you do? You have a most beautiful house, Mrs Tremayne.'

She was walking through a nightmare. She had to be. It was the only explanation. Mr Pettigrew was turning a delighted face to her, but its lines were distorted, shifting shape, expanding and contracting at will. Nancy shut her eyes tight, trying to steady her vision. When she opened them again, the agent had stopped smiling. He was saying something, his voice seeming to come from far away. Then it was booming in her ear.

'Are you all right, Mrs Tremayne?'

Nancy wanted to yell, to scream at him that his wonderful new client was a man who had tried to murder her. Was still out to murder her. But the words wouldn't come. Instead, she stammered out, 'I'm fine, Mr Pettigrew. I missed my breakfast this morning. I think I should eat.'

'Yes, yes, of course. We will leave you in peace. Mr March?' He put out his hand to guide his client to the front door.

But not before March had turned back to say, 'The house is ideal. I'll be back, you can be sure.'

*

Nancy double-locked the front door behind them and

stumbled into the sitting room, toppling onto the sofa, her legs hunched and her voice emitting a low keening. Her home had been violated. March had been allowed to wander the house at will, his tainted hands touching every surface, his murderous breath filling the air of every room.

It was a long time before she could pull herself together, drag herself to her feet. There was a drumbeat in her head: she must make herself secure, make herself secure. Slowly, she began a tour of the house starting from the basement and working upwards. Every window was checked, every cupboard opened. In the bathrooms, she opened the shower doors, in the bedrooms, she crawled beneath the beds. She checked and rechecked anywhere March could have wreaked mischief.

Eventually, she made it to the top floor, the apartment in which Archie had lived for many years. For months, Nancy had avoided climbing this last flight of stairs, but there could be no escape from it now. It would be the very place that March would set a trap.

Archie's rooms were cold and empty, feeling as bleak as her heart. The rocking chair and solid oak desk had gone to his new address, she supposed, the windows bare of the bright blue curtains Morwenna Jago had made for her son. Nancy walked out onto the landing and towards the exit that led to the fire escape. The fire door had stayed locked, it seemed.

As a trial, she grasped the door handle—usually stiff and unforgiving—but this time it moved easily beneath a light touch. A rush of cold air hit her squarely in the face. This, then, was to be March's next move.

# Chapter Eleven

Nancy couldn't sleep. A new pattern of terror was unfolding: first the wreath to tell her that Philip March knew she was unprotected; then the broken bowl to remind her how many precious possessions of hers he'd already broken; then the wasps. They'd been designed to harm, but not to kill. Not yet—he'd been toying with her still. But the open door to the fire escape? Perhaps a signal that the end game was in sight.

Restlessly, she shifted from one side of the bed to the other, then padded several times to the bathroom and back. Switching on the bedside lamp, she sat for a while, propped against the pillows. When she could no longer hold her eyelids open, she turned off the light and, just beginning to doze, slid down into the bed. It was a while before she heard the noise. The bedroom she and Leo shared overlooked a long, narrow garden, which itself abutted a neighbour's in the road running parallel to Cavendish Street. Traffic hum was always audible, but a low hum rather than a noise that disturbed. For central London, this was a quiet house.

The first intimation Nancy had of something, of someone, close by, was a faint slap against the side of the house. It had begun to rain around midnight, she'd noticed the splashes on the window pane when she'd gone to the bathroom last, and the slap, she was sure, was a footstep. A footstep on a wet fire escape that ran past her bedroom and down into the garden. The gate that led to the street was always kept locked, but how difficult would it be to climb over? Or over the neighbour's garden wall? Not difficult at all in the middle of the night without witnesses, and with determination. And Philip March had determination.

Nancy lay straight in the bed, her outstretched limbs taut, her breathing shallow. Waiting, waiting. The slap of a foot came again, just outside her window or so it seemed. She slid out of bed, searching in the dark for anything that could be used as a weapon. Why hadn't she thought of that before she'd gone to bed? The act of locking the fire exit had lulled her to the possibility of a night-time threat. What would March do when he found himself unable to use the door? Break it down? No, it was too sturdy. Break a window? That was much more likely. Her bedroom window.

Silently, she glided to her dressing table, opening the top drawer inch by inch and fumbling inside to find her manicure set. A pair of scissors, too small but sharp. They would have to do. She pressed herself against the bedroom wall, sheltering in the lea of the large oak wardrobe, and waited. Her ears had become sensitive to the slightest sound and when she heard it again, that slight slap of a shoe on the wet iron stairway, she tensed herself for what was to come.

Minutes passed and nothing. Her heart sounded in her ears. Surely he must hear it, too. But was that a duller sound? Further away, then a creak—the gate. He was climbing over the gate. He was going away. She breathed out long and deep, her shoulders slumping, her body feeling so insubstantial that it hardly seemed to exist. He'd gone, but it wouldn't be for long. Climbing back into the bed, she buried herself deep in the covers and tried to sleep again.

*

When Nancy woke, it was past nine o'clock. Wrapping herself in Leo's dressing gown, she walked slowly down the stairs, unsure of what she would find, but the house rested peacefully in a winter sun that was filtering faintly through the curtains. In the kitchen, she made tea and poured herself a bowl of cornflakes, subsiding wearily onto a stool as though she'd already done a day's work. She ate breakfast hardly tasting it, her mind too busy with what she was facing. On impulse, she dumped her empty bowl in the sink and, picking up the telephone, dialled Rose's number. She was lucky. Her friend was at home. It was the one day of the week that Rose didn't work.

Nancy's words tumbled over themselves as she poured out to Rose the fear she felt.

'Did you get to speak to Archie?' Rose asked. When Nancy didn't answer, her friend continued, 'You should, you know.'

There was a silence before Nancy burst out, 'I did. I did speak to him. It was probably the worst thing I could have done.'

Rose's sigh at the end of the phone was audible. 'Then pack a bag,' her friend said decidedly, 'and come and stay with us. You'll be safe here.'

It was a tempting offer, but it was unfair to impose on Rose's family for more than a few days, and afterwards she'd have to come back to Cavendish Street. March was patient. He'd wait for her return.

'Thank you, Rose. That's really kind. Maybe I'll visit when I'm packed. There's a lot to do here and I haven't really started.'

'I can come over and help today,' her friend offered.

Nancy was about to leap at the suggestion when she remembered Dominic Gray. It was today she was having lunch with him. She could put him off, she supposed, but that would mean telephoning Abingers and who might she get at the other end of the line? She couldn't face the likely embarassment. If she telephoned the restaurant—she had its number on the card Gray had given her—it would be letting him down at the very last moment. There was no help for it. Much as she longed for Rose's company, she would have to go to the lunch.

'I need to go out later,' she said, deliberately vague, 'but I'd love some help on another day if you can manage it.'

'I'm free every Wednesday. Just give me a ring and I'll come. But what about you and this dreadful man? You need to go to the police, Nancy.'

'What can I tell them?' she asked desperately. 'It 's the old story. I have no proof of any wrongdoing. I found a broken bowl in my dustbin—the housekeeper could have broken it and said nothing.'

'But the wasps?'

'Wasps build nests everywhere. Why not in a wardrobe that hasn't been used for months? And the door to the fire escape being unlocked? Mr Pettigrew could have opened it to show a client—there's a good view of the garden from there—and forgotten to close it. In any case, Philip will have the agent lined up as a witness to his good intentions. He'd wanted to buy the house, he'd say, not break into it, and Mr Pettigrew would vouch for him. I can see the whole story unfolding. You can be pretty sure I'd be dismissed as a neurotic.'

'You need to sell as soon as you can. Get out of that house and move where Philip March can't find you.'

'I've found somewhere I think might work, a small house in Hampstead. I'm seeing it tomorrow.'

'That's good news. I wish I could come with you, but I'll be back at work.'

'It's fine. I'll let you know what I decide.'

'Do please. And keep safe.'

If only, Nancy thought, as she replaced the receiver. She went upstairs to dress, conscious that what she'd said to Rose was true. She had a house to pack up and so far she had done very little. A plan was forming in her mind. If the agent sold her house within the next few days as he'd suggested, she could pack everything she intended to keep and put it in storage until she had a house of her own. Before then, she might rent a flat on a short term lease, somewhere March couldn't find her. Or accept Rose's invitation and stay a short while, then swallow her misgivings and go down to Penleven. She was due to visit Cornwall for Leo's memorial service, but possibly she could go a little earlier. Anything to get out of Cavendish Street.

The plan galvanised her into making several telephone calls, the first to contact an auction house. She chose Donnellys rather than Abingers, and an appointment was arranged with them to view everything that had to be sold—all of Leo's valuable furniture and most of the antiques. Next, she found a local removal firm, who promised to deliver packing boxes in a day or so and, when she was ready, to collect and store them for her.

For the first time since Leo's death, she seemed in charge of her life and it felt good. Taking control, though, had made her late, and she ended up rushing to get ready for her lunch at the Bagatelle. After Archie's warning, she'd had uncomfortable thoughts about Dominic Gray, wondering if he could in any way be connected with the things that had happened in the house. But it was foolish to think so. He had no grudge against her, unlike Philip. It was Philip March who was threatening her, no one else.

The restaurant was situated close to Abingers, but she

walked to it in a roundabout way, and managed to avoid anyone she knew from the auction house. Dominic Gray was already there and rose to greet her, smiling broadly.

'You found it! It's lovely to see you, Mrs Tremayne.'

'I think it could be Nancy?'

'Nancy it is. Such a pretty name.' He pulled out a chair for her. 'Can I get you a drink?'

'Water would be fine, thank you.'

'A glass of wine with the meal perhaps?'

'I don't think so. I didn't sleep well and I've a bit of a headache.'

'I'm sorry you're not feeling too good. Is moving house proving a worry?'

'I had a bad night, that's all. It happens sometimes.'

He sounded so kind, she was tempted to tell him what had been going on, but decided in the end to keep her own counsel. She still hardly knew him. Maybe if they spent more time together in the future…

The lunch he suggested was light but delicious: cheese soufflé and salad followed by a slice of Baked Alaska. They were finishing their main course when Dominic said, 'Dare I ask how the house sale is going?'

She answered readily enough. 'Very well, I believe. I expect to hear definitely from the agent today or tomorrow. Mr Pettigrew seems certain he has a customer.'

'And Hampstead?'

Nancy smiled. 'Progressing. I have a house to view. If the legal stuff can be tied up quickly, I should be able to move in a few weeks.'

'Wonderful. Now how about a liqueur with your coffee?'

'Just coffee, I think.'

'Have you thought what you'll do after you've bought your new home?'

Nancy was puzzled. 'I'll be working at the studio. I called in there yesterday and it's all fixed. I'll be going back very soon.'

'You'll be working for pleasure then?'

Meaning, she thought, there won't be any need for you to work. It was a refrain Nancy was used to, as though women were expected to retire from the world as soon as they decently could—once they'd snaffled a husband or inherited sufficient money, as she had. A notion so ingrained in society that women continuing to work because their job fulfilled them, was almost impossible to comprehend.

'It's good to work, whatever the reason.' He'd been studying her face and was quick to conciliate. 'Good to keep busy. I really meant—I'm not sure how to put this without sounding insensitive, but your new home… it won't be that costly, I imagine, and you'll have a fairly large estate to deal with afterwards.'

'I suppose so.'

She wasn't sure where the conversation was leading, but Dominic was right. Every day brought closer the decisions she would eventually have to make. Apart from moving house, she'd managed so far to push the idea of inheritance to the back of her mind.

'I've made a start,' she told him. 'Donnellys are coming to value the furniture and paintings. I thought it best not to involve Abingers.'

'You're absolutely right. Keep things nicely separate. But that's really what I was talking about. You'll be a wealthy woman and I wondered if you'd thought how you might deal with it. Or how Leo would want you to deal with it.'

Nancy was taken aback. 'How do you think he'd want me to deal with it?' she asked sharply.

'I'm sorry. I've no wish to upset you, but a conversation

with Mr Harker the other day got me thinking.'

'Yes?'

'He had news of a new gallery being set up. One that would be dedicated to showing the work of women artists. Female painters aren't that bankable, you'll know that well enough, and the gallery is going to need investment, according to Harker.'

'I know nothing about investment.'

'Nor me. But even if I did, I couldn't manage a single pound on my salary, but when Mr Harker talked about it, I thought of you. He said how interested you'd always been in promoting female artists and that Abingers didn't do enough in that direction. He showed me the plans and, I must say, the gallery looks good.'

'A gallery?' Nancy was intrigued. 'Where would it be?'

'By the river, in Wapping. I don't know the area well, but I did go and look at the spot where they're intending to build. It's a vast space and there'll be wonderful river views from the gallery windows.'

'Who is building it?'

'I'm not sure of the actual builders, but a group of investors are funding it. People like yourself, interested in promoting female artists. Currently, they're raising money to go ahead. The land has been purchased and the plans drawn up, so they're fairly far on.'

'It sounds a worthwhile project, but... how exactly do I come into it?'

'All I was thinking, Nancy, was that if you had spare money and wanted to do some good, a bit of philanthropy, you know, this new gallery might be of interest.'

She said nothing for a while, turning the idea over in her head.

'I can always introduce you to the main man,' Dominic

continued. 'It was his idea originally, but he's well-connected and has managed to gather three, maybe four, like-minded spirits to invest with him.'

'Who is he?'

'Leonard Armitage. Do you know him?'

'I've never met him, but of course I've heard of him. I think Leo shared a platform with him once—at some symposium or other. He's a big name in the art world.'

'Exactly. Which is why I think the project will fly. But don't let's talk about it now. Just let me know if you fancy an introduction. Ah, here's our coffee.'

*

She left Gray outside the restaurant and walked slowly back to Cavendish Street. It had been an enjoyable lunch. Dominic was very good company, and he'd introduced a whole new idea to her. Nancy had never before had money to spare, and she'd not allowed herself to think much further than selling the house and furniture and moving to a smaller home. But a gallery specifically for women artists sounded the kind of project she would love. Once the house move was settled, she'd take up the offer of an introduction to Professor Armitage and discover exactly what was involved.

The telephone was ringing as she opened the front door. For a moment, her heart contracted painfully. Telling herself not to be stupid—was she going to feel like this every time the phone rang?—she picked up the receiver.

It was Mr Pettigrew. 'Good news, Mrs Tremayne,' he said, his voice frothing with pleasure. 'My client from New York has confirmed he wishes to go ahead.'

'And Mr March?' she asked nervously.

'I've heard nothing from him. Between you and me, I'm not sure he was a serious buyer. But Mr Dunstable is keen to move in as soon as possible. He is flying into London tomorrow and his family will follow in a few days. He intends to sign the contract as soon as it arrives. Should I contact your solicitor for you, Mrs Tremayne? We have spoken together, started the ball rolling as it were, and I believe he has already prepared a draft contract with only the purchase price missing.'

'It will be a quick sale then?'

'Very quick. And there's good news on the sale price, too. Mr Dunstable is willing to go to four and a half thousand pounds, as long as he can move in immediately.'

Nancy sat down heavily on one of the cushioned ottomans that lined the hall.

'That's more than—'

'I know,' Mr Pettigrew interrupted, almost crowing. 'He is most eager to settle the purchase. We should be able to complete the day after we exchange contracts.'

When she'd put the phone down, Nancy sat and stared for at least ten minutes at the small Renaissance bronze opposite. Four and a half thousand pounds. It was a sum so foreign to her that it hardly made sense. One thing was clear, though. Dominic Gray had been right to say that she should think what to do with her new-found wealth. A gallery for women artists? The idea was enticing.

# Chapter Twelve

Nancy woke the next morning in good spirits. She had never felt so faint-hearted as she had these last few weeks, but yesterday had given her a much-needed lift. She wasn't sure why, but sometimes these days she hardly recognised herself. Maybe it was the sheer fatigue of looking after a very sick man for months, the tiredness finally catching up with her, or the sadness of finally losing him. Maybe it was the fact that she was once more alone in the world and newly vulnerable.

But she was tough, she told herself. From a young age, she'd found the determination, the inner strength, to follow a path of her own choosing, despite the myriad obstacles in her way. And since marrying Leo, she'd found a different kind of strength, one she had used in the service of others. She had taken on people in power and won, seen justice done where it had been absent—faced danger, even death, to succeed.

Another chapter was beginning now, and things would change. She would change. The Cavendish Street house was sold but for the legal niceties, and today she was viewing the house she hoped to make her home. She would find friends in this new world. In some way, she already had. Dominic Gray, when he worked for Leo, had hardly featured in her life. He'd come to Cavendish Street a few days a week and for much of that time she had been away from home, working at the studio. When she'd finally given up her job to care for Leo, her husband had been too ill to do any work and Dominic had faded from sight.

It had been a revelation to find him a sympathetic listener and a pleasant companion. To find him concerned for her future—the new gallery he'd talked of was a scheme with huge appeal. It was the kind of development she'd wanted to champion when she was powerless to do so. That was no longer the case, and she was touched that Mr Harker had recalled the several conversations she'd had with him and remembered her interest. A new home, a new interest, and a return to the studio and the job she loved. Today the future looked brighter than it had for a long time.

Michael Holliday's *The Story of My Life* was playing on Housewives' Choice and, singing along with it, Nancy cleared the breakfast things, then set about finding her raincoat and umbrella. Most days, it had been cold and frosty and she'd not used either since the funeral, but this morning the sky was grey and rain threatened.

Dressed for the stormy day ahead, she opened the front door to find a uniformed man mounting the front steps. He had a wreath in his hands and, behind him parked at the kerbside, Nancy saw a green van belonging to a firm called Blossom House.

He looked up as the front door opened. 'Mrs Tremayne?'

'Yes, but—'

'I have a delivery for you.'

Nancy put out her hand, as though to stop him coming closer. 'I think there's been a mistake. The funeral was several weeks ago. My husband's funeral.' Her voice wavered slightly.

The man fumbled in his overalls pocket and brought

out a white sheet of paper. He shook his head. 'Twenty-two Cavendish Street, name of Tremayne. It's here in black and white. The wreath is definitely for you.'

When she continued to look bewildered, he said in a kindly voice, 'Maybe someone got the wrong date.'

'It would seem so,' she agreed. For a moment, a wave of sadness obliterated her earlier happiness.

The man scratched his head. 'I'm really sorry, missus. I've never had a situation like this and it's a bit awkward. I get paid for each delivery and I've a dozen others to get through this morning... you could always use the flowers for a display,' he said hopefully.

Nancy could see the man was in difficulty and, concerned she'd be late for her appointment in Hampstead, she made up her mind. 'Give it to me,' she said. 'There's obviously been a mix up.'

'Thanks, lady. And sorry again...' He left it at that.

Sorry if it brought back difficult memories, but she wouldn't let it. If she could salvage the flowers as the delivery man suggested, they would brighten the house for a few days. She walked back into the hall and laid the wreath on the satinwood console table. She would try her hand at flower arranging when she returned. But who on earth could have got it so wrong? It would be one of Leo's clients, almost certainly. There were so many of them, busy men with secretaries to do their bidding. One such secretary must have been instructed to send a wreath and mistook the date.

She glanced idly down at the label attached to the wire. No sender's name, it appeared, but the message... the message...

*My greatest sympathy on the loss of Nancy, a once truly beautiful woman,* she read.

She dropped the label as though it had burnt her fingers. Then picking up the wreath, her heart pounding, she hurtled down the stairs to the kitchen and out into the courtyard, tossing the flowers unceremoniously into the dustbin.

Philip March. He wasn't giving up. But she would win this war, build a new life and free herself from him forever. It was time to make a start and leave for Hampstead.

The post had arrived while she'd been downstairs. Several bills, an invitation to a gentleman's club which made her smile, a handbill announcing a sale at the local church and a brown envelope addressed to her. Even without opening it, Nancy knew it was a threat. The envelope, bland and anonymous, had arrived on cue. It was unlikely to contain anything dangerous, but even so she opened it carefully. Inside was a page cut from today's newspaper, *The Times,* no less. Obituaries. She unfolded the paper and scanned the notices. The one eulogising Nancy Tremayne was halfway down the page.

*A young woman in her prime,* she read, *the death particularly sad as it is barely a month since Mrs Tremayne's husband, the highly respected Professor Tremayne, passed away after a long illness.*

The writer was restrained and sympathetic, briefly sketching the outlines of Nancy's life and hinting delicately that her death could well be the result of a broken heart. Philip March was a journalist who could write, she thought, her heart clenched in anger. But it wasn't a broken heart that Mrs Tremayne was due to die of. It was a broken body. Death had stalked Nancy for years, and the wreath and the obituary suggested that today it had arrived on her doorstep. Was March out there now, waiting for her to leave?

The doorbell rang, seeming a confirmation. Of course, he was there. The bell was summoning her to finish the drama that had started on Coronation Day almost five years ago. She had deceived herself into thinking that things could change. Nothing would change. She could refuse to open the door, pack a bag and escape through the courtyard, but to where? He would find her wherever she hid. There was a terrible inevitability about it. This cat and mouse existence would continue until March had exacted the revenge he sought. Why not open the door and brave what was ahead?

Putting the obituary aside, she picked up her favourite handbag and, figure erect, strode to the door. Flinging it wide, she was surprised to feel tears streaming uncontrollably down her cheeks.

Archie Jago stood on the top step, looking bewildered. 'What is it? What's the matter?'

'It's you!' She brought out the words with difficulty, her breath short and irregular.

'Yes, it's me. Who did you… him?'

Nancy backed into the hall and, picking up the newspaper cutting, silently passed it to him. His eyes scanned the page and his expression hardened.

'There's a wreath, too,' she said. 'In the dustbin.'

'The bastard! Here.' Archie took a clean handkerchief from his pocket and handed it to her.

Wiping away the tears, she felt such joy at seeing him, that sensible words failed her. All she could manage was a stuttering, 'Why are you here?'

'I've a day off—the reward for working overtime to finish Harker's wretched catalogue—and I fancied a walk.'

'To Cavendish Street?'

'Why not? It stretches the legs.'

She didn't believe him. She felt certain that Archie had been checking on the house. Had he been keeping watch ever since they parted outside Charlie's café?

'Did you see him? Did you see March?'

'I must have done, though I didn't recognise him. There was this bloke posting an envelope through your door. It seemed a bit odd—the man looked no better than a tramp and I was suspicious. Remember Cornwall? The anonymous letter you received,' he added quickly. There were aspects of Cornwall that neither of them dared remember. 'I thought I'd ring the bell and find out what was going on.'

She gestured to the cutting that Archie had abandoned on the console table. 'Now you know. He was here yesterday, too, when I got back from the studio. Actually inside the house, pretending to be interested in buying.'

'Presumably to check the layout?'

She nodded. 'The estate agent let him roam around on his own and he unlocked the fire exit, so he could gain entry later. Luckily, I found it open before I went to bed. He still came, though. I heard him in the night. Footsteps on the fire escape.'

Nancy had managed to stay calm until this moment, but at the thought of last night's terror, her voice broke and she could feel the tears surge again.

'You need strong coffee,' Archie said practically. 'Come on, I'll make you some.' He made for the basement stairs, leaving her to follow.

'No alcohol!' she called to him.

'Would I do that?'

Archie knew his way around the Cavendish Street kitchen without thinking and, in minutes, had two mugs of coffee steaming on the table. 'Pity about the ban on alcohol. You could do with a tot, and I could do with a few slices of toast. I didn't have breakfast. But best not. You were on your way out and it will make you late.'

'I'm going to be late for my appointment anyway.' Nancy opened the bread bin. 'You're in luck—half a loaf.'

'Meeting Dominic again?'

'If you're going to carp, there's no toast.'

He held up his hands in surrender while she buttered

two slices and searched for the marmalade, finding it on the unreasonably high shelf that Mrs Brindley must have favoured.

Archie took the plate from her. 'Thanks. This will go down a treat. I wasn't about to carp. Just interested if you enjoyed your lunch with the gorgeous Gray.'

'It was nice. It was pleasant to talk to someone I hardly know, to forget my worries for an hour.'

'So another lunch today?'

'No. I'm house viewing, which reminds me that I better telephone and ask the agent to meet me later than we'd arranged.'

'I won't keep you.' He frowned. 'I didn't know you were moving. Where are you going?'

'Hampstead, I hope. I've found a house I think might work for me.' She finished her coffee and put the cup down slowly. She was thinking hard. 'I don't suppose…' she said… 'I don't suppose you'd like to come with me?'

It was a foolish suggestion, but the thought of being with Archie, if only for a few hours, restored some of the courage she'd lost.

Dusting the toast crumbs from his hands, he took his empty plate to the sink. 'Another walk, on the Heath, with all that fresh air?' he said, turning to face her. 'Why not?'

## *Chapter Thirteen*

The Hampstead agent proved helpful, and willing to slot Nancy into his afternoon schedule.

'He'll meet us outside the house at three o'clock,' she said, putting the phone down. 'There'll be plenty of time for a walk.'

'Plenty of time for lunch, too. There's a pub I've been to once or twice—the Holly Tree or something like that. It's an old coaching inn. They do a decent roast, I remember.'

The journey took less than an hour, a walk to Warren Street, followed by a bus ride that left them outside Hampstead Heath Station. By eleven o'clock, they were on the Heath itself and approaching the Mixed Bathing Pool.

'Fancy an open air dip?' Archie asked, a laugh in his voice.

'Not remotely, but if I did, I'd choose the Ladies Bathing Pond. Far more exclusive—and no risk of being drowned by a man who thinks he's Ian Black.'

Circling around the pool, they struck out across the grass, following one of the narrow paths that crisscrossed the Heath. The sky was leaden, growing greyer with every minute, but the view when they reached the top of Parliament Hill was as stunning as any on a day of bright sunshine.

Archie was puffing slightly. 'The highest point in London,' he said, 'and it feels like it.'

'But what a view!' Nancy's focus was on the distant scene. 'Look, the river,' she said, excitedly. 'I can just about see it.' The smallest glimpse of the Thames was visible, winding its sinuous path through a panorama of history. 'St Paul's, too. And the docks—so many cranes.'

'All I can see is smoke. Smoke from a thousand chimneys.'

'Stop complaining! It's wonderful up here.'

'As long as there's a roast at the end.'

Walking side by side, it seemed as though they had never been apart. Archie talked of Abingers, telling her of the forthcoming exhibition and how Mr Harker had been driven half-mad by Aubrey Simmonds' constant changes of mind.

*I think, Harker, we'll include this chap. His work isn't desperately well-known, but that could prove a good selling point. On the other hand...*

Archie's mimicking of the Managing Director in full flow had Nancy laugh out loud. 'You enjoy working there,' she teased. 'Don't deny it.'

'Not for much longer. My contract is strictly temporary.' He paused for a moment while he navigated a bump in the path. 'This house—the one we're going to see—are you sure you want to be all the way out here? It's a much longer journey to the studio. Unless you're intending to give the job up.'

'Definitely not. The journey will be fine and I want to live here. It feels like freedom. The open space, I suppose. And it smells a whole lot better than the middle of London!'

It was Archie's turn to laugh. 'A whole lot better than the East End, for sure.'

They walked for an hour, arriving at Archie's pub in good time for lunch.

'It's called the Holly Bush,' Nancy said. 'You were nearly right.'

'As long as there's—'

'A roast dinner,' she finished for him. 'Hopefully, they'll do a ploughman's, too. I'm not that hungry.'

When Archie had fetched their beer and orange juice from the bar and joined her at a corner table, she asked him the question that had been on her mind for the last few hours.

'Was it a coincidence that you were walking past the house when you saw March this morning?'

'You must know it wasn't. I've been keeping an eye on Cavendish Street, ever since I saw you,' he confessed. 'Hanging around first thing in the morning, then straight after work. Waiting for the bloke to appear. I had to hope he didn't turn up during the day, but I didn't think he would. At this time of the year, evenings and early mornings are pretty dark, so excellent cover for him—full daylight, not so much.'

Before Nancy could respond, the waitress arrived with their order and Archie plunged in to a plate of beef, roast potatoes, brussel sprouts and carrots, temporarily depriving him of speech.

'Had you seen him at the house before today?' she asked, after a while.

'Not a whisper until this morning, and then I didn't recognise him! By then, I'd be waiting around for an hour or so and was just about to give up.'

Nancy put down her knife and fork. 'Why have you been watching?'

'Isn't that obvious? I was worried.'

'But you refused to help when I came to you. Why did you refuse? It made me so angry.'

'*You* made me angry.' He waggled his fork at her. 'You were pretty naïve when I first met you, but I thought you'd learned to judge better, and there you were trusting a complete rotter like Dominic Gray.'

'I don't agree that he is.'

'You'd better. The man is up to no good. Last week he was as edgy as hell, snappier even than usual. He was prying, too, asking me where I lived. I don't know why, but I didn't like it one bit. Then a few days ago, when his phone rang, he banged the office door in my face. I heard snatches of the conversation through the door. He's planning something he doesn't want anyone to know about. *I've done that already*, he told the person on the line. *But we'll have to tackle it differently. I'll sort things out, don't worry*.

'None of it makes sense,' she protested.

'It makes enough sense to tell me that something's not right.'

'Archie.' She reached out and took his hand, feeling its warmth and its strength. 'I think you've got the man wrong. He's been nothing but kind and understanding since Leo died. I believe he wants to be a good friend.'

Archie looked unconvinced.

'It's March who means me harm,' she persevered. 'Not Dominic. He couldn't be clearer that he wishes me a happy future.' She wouldn't mention the investment scheme. Archie would assume immediately that it was some kind of scam, even though Mr Harker and Abingers seemed wholly behind it. Dominic was genuine. He hadn't tried to push her into anything and had promised to introduce her to Professor Armitage, currently one of the most influential people in British art. Archie was simply prejudiced. And Nancy knew how stubborn he could be—he wouldn't change his mind.

*

Nancy loved the house and surprisingly so did Archie. It was just as she'd described to her friend, a roses-round-the-door kind of place. Inside there was a simple layout: two rooms and a small kitchen downstairs, two bedrooms and a bathroom above. A neat square of garden lay at the rear, with a small flower border either side of the front door. Flask Walk itself was delightful and the village shops a few minutes' walk away. Apart from a longer journey to the studio, it was ideal.

'I'll take it,' she said to the agent, as he locked the front door behind them.

For an instant, surprise at such a quick decision showed on his face, then his agent's smooth manner swiftly returned.

'Wonderful news, Mrs Tremayne,' he said, exuding enthusiasm. He gave a small cough. 'And the finance?'

'I'll have sold my house in Marylebone. Next week, I believe. I can exchange contracts on this house immediately afterwards.'

'Wonderful,' he said again. 'But a surveyor perhaps?'

'It's good of you to suggest it, but I don't want one. I just want the house.'

Archie looked across at her, a broad smile on his face.

'Decisive,' he said, when the agent had left them.

'I need to be. These last few weeks, I've been drifting, getting nowhere. I've not even begun packing. Not properly.'

'You'll not get much of Cavendish Street in there,' he remarked, as they walked back to the bus stop, jerking his head in the direction of the house they had left.

'I'm not taking much of Cavendish Street. Just my clothes, a few paintings I like, some of the kitchen equipment and one or two pieces of furniture. The rest is going to auction.'

'Leo spent years collecting that stuff.'

'I know, Archie, and it hurts to think about it. But there's no alternative. I have to move on.'

'You and me, both.'

She knew what he meant.

The bus dropped them back in Warren Street as dusk was falling. 'A cup of tea before you start for home?'

'Good idea. Maybe some cake, too? Lunch has disappeared and I need sustaining.'

'Until you get to Charlie's, I suppose?'

'That is one great caff,' he said, turning to walk beside her.

But when they reached Cavendish Street, disappointment was in store. 'No cake,' she confessed, after a fruitless hunt through the cupboards. 'No biscuits either. There are plenty of eggs, though. I could do them scrambled.'

'Even better.'

'While I get the food, could you go round the house? Just to check. I'm sure it's fine, but the doors, the windows?'

'Under the beds?'

'Yes,' she said crossly. 'And in the cupboards. I have no idea where March will strike next.'

'Sorry. You're right to be anxious. The man needs stringing up.'

When Archie sauntered back into the kitchen whistling, she knew all was well.

'Perhaps he won't try anything more for a while.' She was trying to feel positive. 'Maybe the wreath and obituary were payback for his not being able to break in the other night.'

In her mind, Nancy knew it for a false hope. A payback maybe, but a promise, too. There would be more to come, March's final act.

It seemed that Archie had read her mind. 'How soon before you can get out of here?'

'Mr Pettigrew—don't laugh, he's a very nice man—'

'Is he dainty? He should be with a name like Pettigrew.'

Nancy considered for a moment. 'Yes, he is dainty, but what's more important is that he's sold this house for me for four and a half thousand pounds.'

Archie gaped at her. 'Dainty indeed,' he said, tackling his scrambled eggs with gusto.

'He's rushing ahead with the contract, too. Once I've signed it and Donellys have collected the furniture and paintings, I'm thinking of staying with Rose for a while. I didn't want to intrude and I won't stay that long, but she's adamant it's the right thing to do.'

'Sounds sensible to me. And the Hampstead house?'

'I'll come back to London when the new contract's ready. If it takes longer than I expect, I can always stay at a hotel until moving day.'

'With four and a half thousand pounds, you can stay at the Ritz every night.'

'I won't be doing that. I'll choose something small and out of the way. A place where March won't think to look.'

'It's a pity Mrs B isn't around any more. She could have moved in with you for a while. That would have put the fear of God into March.'

'Much more likely to put it into me. Really, I'm better off without Mrs Brindley's company.'

'She was a battleaxe,' he agreed, 'but she loved Leo.'

'I know that too well. It's the reason she never accepted me. She was kind after Leo died, but the sympathy didn't last too long.'

'What's that about a leopard and its spots?'

'Perhaps none of us ever change,' she said, turning round from stacking the clean plates. 'I haven't.' And Archie hadn't either, she thought.

'People might not change, but circumstances do,' he said simply.

'I know. I wish they didn't. This situation—it's …'

'Insurmountable?' he offered. 'I think that's the right word.'

She walked over to him and placed her two fingers against his lips. 'Sadly, it is,' she whispered.

He bent his head and kissed her on the cheek, but seized by an impulse she couldn't control, she took his face in her hands and kissed him hard on the lips. If that was the last kiss they would ever have, she wanted it to matter.

It wasn't the last. His arms wrapped her close and he was kissing her back. Over and over again. How they arrived in the sitting room she had no idea but, clinging fast, they shed clothes and tumbled together onto the thickly tufted carpet.

Archie gave a faint laugh. 'Thank God for Persian rugs,' he said into her ear, 'though I doubt the weavers had this in mind.'

# Chapter Fourteen

Archie left the house early the next morning. Cavendish Street appeared to be sleeping still, but Archie was suspicious. March could easily be close by and he wondered if he should linger a while, in case the scoundrel showed his face. He'd knock him down the basement steps, if he did, not caring who saw—the milkman on his round, the children's nanny from two doors down, the stiff-collared clerk Archie had seen several times on his way to the office.

March would be back very soon, he knew—the wreath and the obituary suggested as much—and he wanted to be ready for him. He should have pushed the lunatic off the cliff when he'd had the chance, but how could he have known the bloke's obsession was so strong he'd return to complete the job he'd left unfinished that April day?

With work to go to and the clock ticking, Archie knew he couldn't stay around for long. If he'd been able, he would have guarded Nancy every hour of every day but, to do that, he'd have to move in with her—and that wasn't an option. Last night should never have happened. He'd heard that refrain before, he thought wryly, but maybe yesterday it had been inevitable. To spend the day with her, to walk, to talk and laugh with her, had been like coming home. Last night, he'd felt nothing but exhilaration. Now, though, there was sadness. Leo had been dead for less than a month and it seemed to Archie that he had taken his wife from him—again.

How would Leo feel if he knew? His employer's words in Rio, spoken from a hospital bed, were lodged deep in memory. It was clear that at the time his boss had thought he might not return home alive. Avoiding Archie's eyes, he'd looked hard at the counterpane and said, *if anything should happen to me... you'll be beside her, won't you?*

At the time, Archie had read a more profound meaning into Leo's words. *Be beside her*, stay with her forever, make her yours. It had taken him a while to realise he'd been wrong. Leo had never accused him of playing false, but the man had been so obviously jealous, so cutting in his remarks, that Archie had come to think that all he'd been asked to do, if the worst were to happen, was to ensure Nancy's safe return to England.

A year later and Leo was dead, but Archie knew he must keep his distance, if only for Nancy's sake. She was grieving, she was vulnerable, and though he knew she loved him, he also knew she would feel nothing but pain if he forced her to push Leo out of her life. That was no basis for a happy future—for either of them.

Today was his last day at Abingers, though he hadn't mentioned it to Nancy. She would have asked him what he intended to do next, and he simply didn't know. He supposed the agency would come up with another posting, if he contacted them, but he wasn't sure he wanted to. He'd enjoyed working at the auction house. It was akin to the work he'd done for Leo, not as responsible, but interesting in its own way. He'd enjoyed being back in the world of art. He knew where he was in it. To return to the bread and butter jobs the agency would have on their books was uniniviting. He thought again of returning to Cornwall, of trying to find work other than in fishing, the only likely source of income in Port Madron. But the thought was fleeting—to go back would be admitting defeat.

There was a need in him, though, to get away somewhere, anywhere, and leave Nancy to sell the old house and make her move to Hampstead. He could see her living in that cottage very happily and enjoying the job she'd trained for. It would be a good life for her, as long as that scoundrel, March, disappeared for good.

Maybe, in time, they would meet again and recognise their feelings hadn't changed. Maybe, then, there'd be a chance for them, though it seemed an improbable outcome. She would meet someone else. With four and a half thousand pounds, her choice would be wide, he thought savagely. Then castigated himself for believing that Nancy would succumb to that kind of man. Yet she thought Gray was a decent chap… and he almost certainly wasn't.

*

'Archie stayed last night,' Nancy told her friend on the telephone that evening.

'And?' Rose's voice sounded expectant.

'And it shouldn't have happened,' she said in a low voice.

'Why do you say that, Nancy? Is it because you're worried what people will think? You mustn't let others judge you. I certainly wouldn't criticise, and neither would anyone else with half a heart.'

There was a long silence, until Rose added, 'I thought Archie was special to you.'

'He is. He always has been, but Leo deserves better. I never really told you…' Her voice faltered. 'I never told you how disloyal I'd been. I betrayed Leo once and swore never to do it again. But I did. Last night.'

'Nancy,' her friend said gently, 'your husband isn't with you any longer, so how can you betray him?'

'It makes no difference. Leo would be angry if he knew what I'd done. Bitterly upset. And he'd hate me for it. It's not other people's judgement I'm afraid of, it's Leo's.'

There was another long pause before Rose spoke again. 'You're not going to like this, but I think you're being plain silly. Leo loved you. I know your marriage had problems, but he loved you, and what man who cared deeply for his wife wouldn't want her to be happy?'

'I've told myself that, but it doesn't work. Leo will always be there between us. I feel it and I know Archie feels it, too. When he said goodbye this morning, I knew it was the last time I'd see him for a long time. Maybe forever.'

Nancy heard a sharp intake of breath at the other end of the line. Exasperation, perhaps?

'I can't see why you can't make it together. Leo doesn't always have to be there—you could persuade him to go away—when you're ready.'

'Perhaps I'm not then.'

Rose was a dear friend, but they were never going to agree on something so fundamental to Nancy's understanding of herself. And she couldn't expect it.

'How's the house sale going?' Rose asked, returning to a less awkward subject.

'I signed the contract this morning! The solicitor actually came to the house, he was so keen to hurry things along. Mr Dunstable—he's the man buying Cavendish Street—signed his copy a few days ago and sent it on to his solicitor in London. Apparently, the contracts are being exchanged some time today. The buyer is flying in from New York over the weekend and the sale itself will go through early next week.'

'That is swift,' Rose said admiringly. 'And once it's done,

you'll come to us?'

'If that's okay with you. I wonder... could I stay a week? By then, I might be the owner of a new home.'

'You must stay as long as you want. Let me know what train you're catching and I'll meet you at Wimborne station.'

Tuesday, Nancy calculated. That was when she could leave for Dorset, and Tuesday was only four days away. Replacing the receiver, she felt a rush of relief. Only four days in which March could do his worst, and then she would be away from London and safe. She'd have to return for a day to sign the Hampstead contract, but the visit would be swift, and she'd make very sure the estate agent kept her new address under lock and key.

*

Surveying the collection of half-empty cardboard boxes the next morning, Nancy's heart sank a little. Today, she must buckle down and finish the packing—there was now very little time left. Both the auction house and the removal firm were calling later that afternoon. But only a few minutes into wrapping the paintings and ornaments she intended to keep, the doorbell rang. As always these days, her heart did a nasty somersault at the intrusion, before she breathed deeply and padded down the stairs. Fixing the safety chain in place, she opened the front door a few inches.

'I wondered if you were free today?' Dominic Gray stood halfway down the front steps, smiling up at her.

Nancy felt flustered. Dominic usually telephoned and she hadn't been expecting to see him in person. 'Not really,' she said. 'I've Donnellys coming later this afternoon.'

'But for the next hour or so?'

'Well, no. I should really be packing. There's still a lot to do.'

'The thing is, Nancy, Professor Armitage is in Wapping this morning. He got back early from some conference or other and was keen to do a site visit straightaway. I thought it would be a good chance for the two of you to meet, take a look together at what's being proposed. The Prof is the one who really knows what's what.'

Nancy was torn. The house move seemed to be on wheels now and she'd been keen to pack everything she was taking to Hampstead before Donnellys arrived to collect the goods for auction. That way, there'd be no mistakes. On the other hand, in a few days' time she would have left for Dorset and, with Professor Armitage's busy schedule, another meeting could prove impossible to arrange for months ahead.

'How about it?' Dominic urged. 'I'm due into work myself by three, so you'll get back in good time for Donnellys.'

It was too good an opportunity to miss, she decided, abandoning in the hall the pile of spare newspapers she'd amassed for packing. She grabbed her bag from the sitting room, her thick coat from the bentwood stand, and followed him to the waiting cab.

It took nearly an hour to reach the site in Wapping, crawling for the most part through heavy traffic. Watching the meter tick steadily upwards, Nancy wondered who was paying for this taxi. Knowing how modest salaries were at Abingers, she hoped it wasn't Dominic. While they travelled, Gray unfolded two large sheets of drawings and proceeded to explain the layout of the proposed gallery: the grand foyer—'something to rival the Victoria and Albert'—the shape and size of the main exhibition rooms, the education wing, and the landscaping that would surround the site.

'The idea is that there'll be plenty of outdoor space that people can use in good weather.'

'It sounds wonderful.' Nancy tried to instil enthusiasm

into her voice. They were approaching the site at last, but the area felt too dismal to envisage in any tangible fashion the plans Dominic was expounding.

'I know it doesn't look much at the moment.' He was evidently aware of her struggle to sound positive. 'But it will, I promise. Here will be fine,' he told the cabbie.

As they walked towards the empty expanse lying naked beneath heavy skies, Nancy's gaze travelled to the ribbon of river just beyond. 'What was here before the site was cleared?' she asked.

'Small workshops mainly, a few huts of corrugated iron, that kind of thing. It was crying out for development. Look.' He unrolled the plans again. 'You can see there's enough space for a long walkway in front of the building. I think tree-lined, don't you? And space either side for seating. Wooden benches, maybe. Even a table or two for picnics. Then the rear windows of the building—see how large they're going to be. They'll look out of over the river, so visitors will get double the pleasure. Beauty inside and out.'

'You make it sound a great deal better than it looks.'

'Isn't it always the same with building sites?'

Nancy turned around, looking from right to left. 'So where is Professor Armitage meeting us?'

Gray turned around, too, as though surprised to hear the professor's name. 'He should be here.' He put a hand to his hair and ruffled it. 'The chap must be running late. Let's walk over to the river while we're waiting.'

Nancy fell into step beside him, walking swiftly. It was another cold day, the wintry sun barely warming the surrounding air, and the breeze from the river, icy. They stood for a while by the parapet that guarded a steep fall to the grey waters flowing to the North Sea.

'Which of your favourite painters would you choose to

showcase first?' Dominic smiled down at her.

'I'm not sure. Winifred Nicholson? Vanessa Bell?' She was too cold to think straight. 'Or someone entirely unknown?'

'For my money, I'd make it Laura Knight. To start with at least, someone who's widely appreciated. We could have a grand opening. Champagne, canapés, the great and the good. You know the kind of thing. Really make a splash. Invite the press and get the event reported in the newspapers the next day.'

'It sounds wonderful.' Nancy tried to smile but her cheeks were too stiff. Hugging her arms around her, she said, 'I think I'll have to go, Dominic. I'm just too cold to wait any longer and I've a huge amount to do at home.'

'I'm so sorry. I wonder if Professor Armitage came and left before we arrived?'

'He must have known we were coming.'

Dominic looked uncertain. 'I mentioned it on the telephone, but I was unsure at the time whether or not you were free to come. Armitage may have arrived a bit early, decided you weren't coming and turned tail. I'll have to arrange another meeting.' He stamped his feet against the rock-hard ground. 'It's perishing today, isn't it? How about a quick bite at The Six Bells? That should warm us up. The pub's only a few minutes' walk from here.'

'It's a kind thought, but I really don't have the time.'

'Maybe lunch at the next meeting then.'

'Maybe, though I'm not sure when I can come again. I'm off to Dorset in a few days' time.'

Gray looked surprised. 'Really? I thought your house move would keep you here for a while.'

Nancy had no wish to spell out the danger she faced in London, saying simply, 'I need to get away for a short time.'

A deep crease appeared on his forehead. 'It's possible

I might be able to sort something out before you leave for Dorset, if the Prof hasn't already departed on his travels. I hope you don't feel today has been a complete waste of your time.'

'Of course not. I've seen the site. I've seen the plans. I've a much better idea now how the gallery will look.'

'In the meantime, be thinking about those painters we talked about. And the ceremonial opening. I know it's a long way off, but important people run their diaries a couple of years ahead and it's those we want to attract.'

'I will, I promise. Now, can you point me in the direction of the underground? The traffic is still bad and it will be the quickest way home, I think.'

'I'll walk you to the nearest station and say goodbye there, if that's okay. I've a few errands to run before I head off to Abingers.'

# Chapter Fifteen

Donnellys arrived on the stroke of four that afternoon, the team of men setting to work immediately. They were expert at their job, taking the greatest care with the furniture, most of which was antique, carrying each item carefully down several flights of stairs to the large van waiting at the kerbside. Chests, occasional tables, the high-backed fireside armchairs, a dresser, a secretaire, a four poster bed and two sideboards, were loaded, piece by piece, standing ready for their journey, padded and protected by a stack of thick blankets.

Hard on their heels, a smaller van bearing the Donnellys' nameplate, arrived to carry away the paintings and sculptures. The whole operation took well over two hours, but waving them off from the front steps, Nancy felt relieved to be free of so many possessions. For Leo, they had been precious items collected over many years, but she had always felt weighed down by them, worried she might scratch the polish, break a vase, knock into a sculpture. Even so, walking back through the front door, she felt the house denuded—almost gaunt and unfriendly—and was glad she'd be here for only a few more days.

Shortly after both Donnellys' vans had disappeared along Cavendish Street, the removal firm arrived to collect the storage boxes that Nancy had finally managed to fill. These were *her* precious possessions. It wouldn't be long, she told herself, before she was opening them again, this time in a cottage in Hampstead, and it gave her a good feeling.

Despite the removal men working swiftly, it was late by the time they left and, too tired to think of cooking, Nancy made a cheese sandwich and a pot of tea to take to the sitting room. For a moment, she stood on the threshold, absorbing the transformation. The room seemed ghostly, the curtains still in place and left for the new owner, but only a sofa and a television to fill the large room—the removers would return on Tuesday morning for the remaining furniture once the house was sold. That was the day she'd agreed to move out and head for Dorset.

Switching on the television, she plumped down on the sofa to eat her meagre supper. A new arts programme, *Monitor,* was being broadcast. Leo would have disliked it, she was sure—*too flimsy,* she could hear him say—but she thought it interesting, although not interesting enough to keep her eyelids from gradually closing. Still, she felt a sense of satisfaction, the beginnings of content. It had been a shame to miss Professor Armitage but they would meet eventually. And really there was no rush—she'd need time to decide how best to spend Leo's money when it swelled her bank account as soon as next week. All in all, things seemed at last to be working out and she dared to believe the worst was over.

The next two days promised to be a flurry of activity. There were train times to check, a case to pack, neighbours to bid farewell, and on the Monday morning, some last minute shopping to do, choosing presents for Rose and the children. She didn't want to go to Dorset empty-handed. There had been no sight or sound of Archie and she wondered if he was continuing to monitor the comings and goings in Cavendish Street. Perhaps not. Perhaps he believed, as she was beginning to, that the wreath and the bogus obituary had been enough to satisfy March's madness, at least until Tuesday, when she'd disappear from Marylebone forever. Or maybe Archie had simply walked away, thinking it best for both of them. He'd done it before and, if she hadn't asked him for help, he would have stayed away. She would save them both from more upset, slipping quietly away from Cavendish Street—to Rose and then on to her new life.

On Monday, she was up early and in the Oxford Street shops by nine o'clock, returning home pleased with her purchases. Rose, she thought, would love the embroidered cushions she'd chosen and a helpful saleswoman had suggested presents for both the children. The telephone was ringing as she walked through the front door—her solicitor confirming they would be completing the sale tomorrow, and the money would be in her bank account by noon.

How strange, she thought. Strange and unsettling to realise she would be a wealthy woman. Money would give her choices, choices she'd never had before, and in the next few months she must work out for herself the way she wanted to live. All in all, the world was definitely looking brighter.

It was when she'd settled in a chair with a cup of tea, that she was gripped by sudden guilt. She couldn't do as she'd planned. She couldn't, after all, leave town without telling Archie that she was going. She would push a note through his door, she decided, while he was at work. Easier for them both than meeting face-to-face.

She had dredged a pad of writing paper from the bottom of her suitcase when the telephone rang again. This time it was Dominic Gray.

'How are you, Nancy?'

She murmured something about being busy, but well.

'Splendid,' he said heartily. 'I've good news, I think.

Professor Armitage has just been in touch. He's mortified that he missed us the other day, desperately apologetic, though I think it might have been my fault after all. I couldn't have been clear enough about the time we were getting to the site. Apparently, he went there, waited a while and then gave up on us. But the good news is that he's going again today. How are you placed?'

'I'm ready to leave tomorrow.'

'All done and dusted then?'

Nancy smiled at the phrase. 'All done and dusted,' she repeated.

'The Prof wants to shout us lunch, to make up for the confusion. He's suggested meeting at the Five Bells for a drink and a light meal. What do you think? He could talk to you about the gallery over lunch, then we could go together to the site.'

Nancy was at a loose end until midday tomorrow when the taxi was booked to take her to Paddington station, in advance of Mr Dunstable and his family moving in. It would be possible, she supposed, to drop her note in to Archie on her way to the Wapping site. His flat in Reardon Road was fairly close.

'It sounds good,' she agreed. 'Shall I meet you both at the Five Bells?'

'Splendid,' Dominic said again. Shall we say twelve-thirty?'

After the phone call, she went back to her blank sheet of paper. It took several attempts before she was satisfied with the letter, tussling with herself as to how much she should say. In the end, she wrote a few simple lines:

*Dear Archie*

*Just a brief note to say that Cavendish Street is now sold and Mr Dunstable and his family are moving in tomorrow. I'll be catching the afternoon train to Wimborne and will be staying with Rose for a while. In the meantime, I'm off to meet Professor Armitage for lunch at the Five Bells. I'm sure you'll know the pub—and the professor. I'm hopeful of using Leo's money for a good cause. Wish me luck.'*

*Nancy*

*

Reardon Road was deserted when she arrived, its inhabitants either at work or busy within doors. Finding her way to his house from the bus stop was easy enough, and coming to it for the first time in daylight, she noticed a postbox as she walked up to the front door. It was fixed to the house wall and was presumably for residents to share, then sort the mail between themselves. Now the moment had come, she felt her spirits fall, her heart leaden, but she slid the slim envelope into the box and walked quickly away, refusing to allow herself a backward glance.

*

Archie wasn't due at the new job in Haringey until mid-week—he'd eventually agreed a further contract with the Bloomsbury agency. There were a couple of days still to be filled: lunch at Charlie's maybe, a walk by the river this afternoon, an evening in the pub to follow. It wasn't exactly exciting, but then life wasn't these days. He'd resigned himself to that.

He was coming back from the corner shop, a packet of Player's Navy Cut in his pocket—he seemed to be smoking a whole lot more these days—when he caught sight of Nancy. His chest tightened. Was she coming to see him? He watched as she walked up to his front door, then saw her slide a letter into the communal postbox. She would expect him to be at work, he supposed, but he doubted she would have rung the bell in any case. Like him, she'd decided that distance was best.

Watching her walk swiftly along Reardon Road to join the main thoroughfare, Archie had to stop himself from following. Instead, he strode across the street to his house and fished out the envelope she'd left. It took him a minute to read her note. A second more to be seized by a terrible fear. Professor Armitage was out of the country. Archie knew that for a fact. On his last day at Abingers, he'd been tasked by Mr Harker to contact the man. Armitage was in Russia and when Archie had finally reached him, first by telegram, then by telephone, the professor had apologised for being unavoidably delayed. His plans had had to change and he was now in Moscow for the rest of the month, and very sorry that he'd be unavailable to open the exhibition Abingers was staging.

Who had told Nancy that Armitage would be at the Five Bells? Who had arranged this supposed meeting? Someone who knew the professor was out of the country? There were only three people who did—the news of Armitage's prolonged stay in Russia would not yet have spread beyond Harker's office. Archie knew, Harker knew, and so did Dominic Gray. *He* had to have been the one to send Nancy on this spurious mission. But why?

Too many questions and none of them likely to have a comfortable answer. He had to get to the Five Bells, warn Nancy that she was walking into possible trouble. He turned quickly from the house and ran down the street to the main road, hailing a taxi as he ran. It was the worst decision he could have made. Ten minutes later, sitting on the edge of the scratched leather seat, he counted the yards the taxi had moved, hemmed in as it was by traffic on all sides.

'Better walk, mate,' the cabbie told him.

Walk? It would take too long. A bus would be as bad as the taxi and the underground station lay in the opposite direction. The only thing he could do was run. Run faster than he ever had before.

# Chapter Sixteen

Dominic jumped up to greet her as Nancy walked into the Five Bells, and led her to the table he'd secured, tucked just behind the door.

'It's good to see you, Nancy.' He held her hand just a little too long. 'Thank you for coming at such short notice. Now what will you have?'

'A lemonade will be fine.'

'Nothing stronger?' His eyebrows lifted slightly.

'Not at this time of day. Lemonade is fine.'

'If you insist...'

Dominic elbowed his way to the bar, bringing back a plastic menu along with the drinks.

'Shall we order, do you think? There's not a lot on offer, but fish and chips sounds pretty good.'

She took a sip of her drink. 'Shouldn't we wait for Professor Armitage?'

'Actually, I was wondering if I should order for him, too. They take a while to serve here, but perhaps I'd better not. He might have an aversion to fish.'

'Or chips,' she said smiling. 'Must you be back at Abingers soon?'

'I've the afternoon off. A special concession as I've been working overtime for several days.'

'Another exhibition?'

'No such luck. I've been helping to clear the attics. Do you remember them?'

Nancy remembered them well. It was where she had hidden in such distress after her name had been bandied around the auction house as... as an easy woman. It was where Leo had found and comforted her, where their relationship had truly started.

'I do remember them,' she said. 'A complete jumble. No wonder you had to work overtime.' She took another sip of her lemonade. It was sweet to the taste. 'I've been thinking about the gallery,' she went on, 'seeing the plans in my mind's eye and imagining how it would look in reality.'

'It's difficult to visualise, isn't it? Particularly in this weather when the site looks so bleak.'

'It's why I'm looking forward to talking to the professor. Hopefully, I'll gain a greater insight. What time did you arrange with him?'

Dominic looked up at the Guiness wall clock, a relic of the Festival of Britain. 'He should be here any time now.' He paused. 'There is something, I ought to mention before he gets here.'

'Yes?'

'As I told you, there are several investors like yourself interested in the project, but up until now Mr Harker hasn't been able to attract any really big fish. Anyway, as of this week, we have managed to snare a big beast.'

'Really?' The mixed metaphors made her smile. Dominic was so enthusiastic, it put her to shame.

'I can't say who at the moment, it's all very hush hush, but this company, well, it's big.' He laughed. 'And connected to the art world and willing to spend its cash if it gets sufficient publicity. But—'

'I knew there'd be a "but".'

'They're offering to sign up for half the initial cost, which is quite something.'

Nancy nodded. It had become very hot in the pub. Too many people, she thought. 'That is huge, I agree. So where does the "but" come in?'

'Hang on, I'm getting there! The company has stipulated that before they sign, they need to know there are others willing to find the remainder of the money. I suppose it's only fair. They don't want to be landed in any kind of financial mess.'

'I see.' She took a long drink and thought about it. 'They want names?'

'Names and some kind of subscription, I suppose you could call it. A pledge of future donations.'

'You're talking money.'

'Only a very small amount,' he said hastily. 'Small for you, at least, now you've sold. A cheque for five pounds. Or maybe seven. Something like that.'

'Well, which is it?'

The pub had filled up considerably since she'd arrived and the noise and heat was making Nancy feel dizzy. She took another drink.

'To be honest, I'm not absolutely sure. But if you give me a cheque, I can fill it in once I know.'

'You want me to sign a blank cheque?' She looked at him in amazement, trying hard to focus on his face.

'If it's a problem, I could telephone you in Dorset with the amount and you can send me or Mr Harker a cheque through the post. There is a time limit, though. The company I'm talking about won't go ahead unless they have the surety within the next few days, so it's pretty urgent. And I don't know about you, but I'm always a little wary of sending cheques through the post. I just thought if you gave me a cheque now, I could fill it in and secure your place on the investors' list. And, of course, secure the future of the gallery.'

Nancy hesitated, feeling a hot sweat creep up from her feet and spread through her entire body.

'You don't trust me?'

'It's not that,' she said, though she knew it sounded feeble. What else could it be but a lack of trust?

'Leo trusted me,' he said stiffly. 'Abingers trust me. And I thought we were friends.'

He was right. She was being unfair. She reached for her handbag, looking for her cheque book. Banking was relatively new to her. She had never had an account until she'd begun the job at the studio and then only because pay came as a monthly cheque rather than the weekly envelope she'd known at Abingers. It had been difficult to set up. The bank manager had been scandalised, but Leo had insisted she had her own account and stood guarantor for her. When it was done, she'd felt inordinately proud of the cheque book she was holding in her hand.

'Here, take my pen,' Dominic said.

'It's fine. I have my own.' She looked across at him, her gaze fuddled, but when her eyes caught his directly, he looked down at the table. Dating and signing the cheque, she tore it off and handed it to him.

'Thank you.' He folded it into his inside pocket with a smile. 'I'll let you know the exact sum as soon as I've checked properly. Do I have your telephone number in Dorset?'

'I'll write it down for you.'

She was fumbling in her handbag again, looking for the small notepad she always carried, when she became aware that people standing closest to their table were moving to one side, as though to let someone through. She turned her head to see who it was, but found herself suddenly lifted out of her seat. Dominic rose from his chair, his expression confused. She reached out to him, but instead of offering his hand in help, he moved quickly around the table, and grabbed her by the arm. There was another man, a man on the other side of her, though Nancy couldn't see him. He was holding her hard against his body. Between them, the two men began to walk her to the pub door. She tried to pull herself free, but their grip was too strong.

'Everything all right, mate?' she heard one of the drinkers at the bar ask.

'Fine. Just a bit too much to drink.' That was Dominic. 'You know what it is with the ladies.'

The voices came to her tinny and unreal, echoing in the back of her head. She felt close to losing consciousness, but the blast of cold air as the pub door was pushed open revived her slightly and she used every ounce of strength she possessed to stop herself from being dragged away. Dragged to the river. Through dim eyes, she could just make out the ribbon of water. Danger screeched at her and, in one last effort to break free, she kicked out and caught Gray on the shin. He let out a loud howl and momentarily loosened his grip. Struggling hard, she tried to wrestle her arms free, but the second man had her clamped to himself as though in an iron cage. Then she knew. March. Philip March. There was a darkness filling her head and then there was nothing.

*

She came round on the paved river walk, a stiff breeze stirring her awake, and found herself pinned on either side, her back against the parapet where she'd stood only days ago.

Her throat felt as though she'd swallowed broken glass, and she struggled to speak. 'Dominic?' she said faintly. 'You know this man?' What a stupid question. Of course, he must know him.

March swung round, pushing his face into hers. 'Your friend, Nancy, is mine, too. Fancy that! I needed help and Gray was just the man for the job. He spins a good yarn, doesn't he?'

'My head,' she mumbled. 'The lemonade. What did you do to it?'

'Sorry about that,' Dominic said. 'Had to be done, I'm afraid. We wouldn't have got you out of the pub otherwise.'

She tried desperately to think through the fog clouding her brain. Think of any way she could escape the fate that was now so close.

'Why am I here?' she asked, though she need not have. What foolishness had made her believe March had disappeared for good?

He pushed her roughly backwards so she was half bent over the parapet. 'Our mutual friend here is a trifle short of money and you have some. Plenty, so I hear.'

'The blank cheque?'

'Stupid girl. But then you always were stupid. Never sign a blank cheque for whatever reason—not that you'll be signing many cheques in future. Gray gets the money, and I get you. Neat, don't you think? When the man you called your husband died, I discovered it was Dominic who'd been working for him, not that thug he used to employ, so I introduced myself. A match made in heaven, wouldn't you say?'

Nancy half turned her head as far as she could, trying to look at Dominic. 'You were happy to deceive me, even though you knew what this lunatic intended?'

'You need to watch your words, Miss Nicholson, or I will make you very sorry. Extra sorry.' March appeared to smile at the thought, and she felt sick seeing it. 'I've had a few weeks' fun tormenting you, but this is where I get my real pleasure. Our little game had to come to an end some time, and today it does. I won't be making the same mistake I did in Cornwall. This time, Nancy, you won't be going home.'

'Steady on,' Dominic Gray interjected. 'Hurting her—killing her?—is not part of the agreement. I'll share the money with you.'

'It's part of *my* agreement. I've no interest in money. This,' and he pointed at Nancy, 'this is what interests me. A woman who is false through and through. For a little while, I toyed with the idea of forgiving her, marrying her at last, now that her supposed husband is dead. But I find I can't. She has given me too much pain, reduced me to nothing. I can't let her live. It wouldn't be fair. It was just the manner of her death I had to decide. And here it is.'

'The river,' she said, knowing it for the truth.

'Got it in one. The Thames is quite deep at this point, I believe. You might swim for a while, if you can, but in this cold, it won't be not for long. And it's a lonely stretch. There'll be no one to save you.'

Nancy didn't need to look to know the riverside walk was deserted and the river itself close to shore, empty.

'Look here—' Gray began, before he was thrust to one side, and Nancy lifted bodily onto the parapet.

In his anger and madness, March seemed to have gained the strength of ten men. Nancy's foot caught on a jagged piece of stone protruding from the wall and she struggled to find a foothold. But, in that instant, she felt a thud in her back and was sent flying, over and down into the rushing waters, her head cracking as she fell, against one of the small boulders that lined the river's edge.

## *Chapter Seventeen*

Archie ran all the way to the Five Bells and arrived hardly able to breathe. As he stood at the pub door, chest heaving and bent almost double, his eyes fixed on the figures he saw in the distance. Two men appeared to be dragging something, someone, between them. Someone being hauled towards the river. As he watched, the previously limp form came to life, lashing out with a foot and kicking one of the men hard. A faint howl came to him through the damp air. What the hell was going on? Then, with a sickening jolt, he realised. It was Nancy!

Reaching into whatever reserves of energy he had left, Archie raced towards the water. Dominic Gray must have heard the pounding footsteps because he looked round, startled at the intrusion. But only for a moment. Archie swung a hefty punch that Gray was unable to dodge. The man crumpled at the knees and fell onto the ground, hitting the paving stones hard, blood pouring from the wound. Archie ignored him, swinging round to pile into March. But it was too late. He heard the splash as he slammed his fist into March's face.

Somehow he found the strength to heave the man to his feet, bundle him onto the parapet and, in a moment of blind fury, thrust him off the wall and into the water. Within a second, Archie had followed, tearing off his coat and clambering onto the barrier to jump into the murky waters. He swam as powerfully as he could towards Nancy's inert body, making a grab for her before she could disappear beneath the surface for a second time.

He had his arms around her, peddling them back towards the shore, but the tide ran strongly here and he found himself drifting out into the open river and away from safety. Water began its insidious creep towards his mouth, but doggedly he kept Nancy's head raised while he sculled to keep them afloat. He was wearying by the second, gradually losing momentum, their drift becoming ever more pronounced. Soon he would lack the strength to keep them safe. If they were to die together, he hoped she knew he was beside her.

Out of nowhere, it seemed, an oar was thrust at him, a voice yelling from somewhere above. Archie stopped sculling and grabbed at the oar, treading water as a pair of arms reached down and disentangled Nancy's limp body from his grip. He felt a sudden lightness and, with both hands now free, he clung to the oar. Now the pair of arms were back, grabbing at his shirt, helping him with his last ounce of energy to scramble up the side of an ancient rowing boat.

'Are you okay, mate? A bit cold for a swim,' their rescuer said, returning to his station at the oar. 'You'll find blankets on the bench beside you.' His fellow rower gave a grunt but said nothing.

Archie wrapped a length of grey felt around Nancy and then took a blanket for himself, huddling down beside her in the well of the boat. He was grateful for the men's apparent lack of interest. Perhaps rescuing drowning people was commonplace for them.

They'd been travelling a few minutes, when their rescuer said over his shoulder, 'Looks like you'll need to get her to hospital. There's a landing stage a little upstream. And a phone box.'

The man's voice seemed to waken Nancy and for the first time she opened her eyes. She didn't speak, but Archie could feel her body shaking against him. He put his arms around her, holding her tightly in an attempt to keep her warm.

Slowly, the boat was rowed back up the river. The shore was close now and Archie could clearly see the landing stage the man had mentioned. Ironically, it was at almost the same spot where they'd entered the water.

'This is where we'll tie up,' their rescuer said, 'and Bert here will telephone for help.'

'Telephone for an ambulance,' Archie said quickly. 'There's no need for the police. It was a silly accident.'

He'd spin a story, if he had to. No one need know the truth. Nancy had climbed on the parapet to get a better view of the river, he'd say, then tripped and fell, hitting her head on the way down. He'd dived in to save her, but then got into trouble until a passing rowing boat had rescued them. The story made them both look a little stupid, but it would stop questions he didn't want to answer. Questions that Nancy wouldn't want to answer either. Gray would be found by a passer-by soon enough—Archie had no interest in knowing whether the man was dead or alive—but if Gray was still breathing, he was unlikely to speak of today's events.

As the boat drew into the small wooden jetty, Archie got to his feet, scanning the river towards Westminster and then back to where the rowing boat had found them. There was no sign of a swimmer. No sign of anyone flailing in the water. March was dead, he thought. At last.

*

Nancy woke to the sound of a medicine trolley being wheeled

to her bedside.

'How are you feeling, young lady?' the nurse asked, bringing the trolley to a halt. 'You gave us a bit of a fright, you know, but you've a much better colour this morning.'

'I'm...' Nancy tried to speak, but the words wouldn't come. 'I'm...'

'Don't talk. Save yourself for the visitor who's waiting to see you.' She shook two tablets from a brown glass bottle and filled a glass of water. 'Aspirins if you need them, but you might not.'

The nurse moved on to the next patient and Nancy closed her eyes again. A visitor? Archie, she thought. It must be Archie. He'd been there, by the river, when she'd tried frantically to find a toe-hold on the parapet, to claw herself back from its edge. She'd heard his voice, heard him cursing. The water below had flowed swiftly, dark and cold. Then she'd been falling... she hadn't been able to stop herself... but his arms were buoying her up, keeping her from the icy water, and she'd known she was safe.

When she opened her eyes again, it was Rose sitting by her bedside.

Nancy's mouth formed an "o" of surprise. 'How did—?'

'Don't talk,' Rose said, echoing the nurse. 'The hospital telephoned me and I came straightaway. Someone must have picked up your handbag and the almoner found my number in your notebook.'

But Archie. She wanted to ask about Archie. Then the whole ghastly series of events came rushing back at her. Dominic Gray and the pub and signing that cheque. She couldn't have been more stupid if she'd been trying for fool of the year. Fool of the century.

'Has anyone told you what happened?' Nancy managed to ask.

'You fell in the river, that's all I know, but your man saved you, then a passing boat rescued you both.'

Your man. How sweet that sounded. 'And Archie—is he okay?'

'I asked, but the hospital don't know. You were the one the ambulance crew brought back, though the nurse I spoke to said they were called out again later—to a spot close by. Someone else, though. Not Archie. There's no record of his being admitted here.'

It must have been Gray the ambulance men had picked up. Dominic Gray. Nancy was seized with anguish.

'Rose, you can't believe how stupid I've been.'

'You're not to upset yourself. Whatever's gone on, it's over. You're safe, and your job now is to get perfectly well.'

'I trusted him,' Nancy continued, unable to free her mind of the catastrophic error she'd made. 'I trusted Dominic Gray. I thought he was a good friend. Archie warned me, but I wouldn't listen.'

'You're not to fret,' Rose said again, taking hold of Nancy's hand and holding it gently. 'At some time or another, we all make mistakes in judging people. It means our trust gets abused, but if we never trusted, we'd never make a friend.'

'It wasn't just bad judgement. I was completely taken in by him.' There had been moments of doubt, Nancy recalled, but she hadn't followed them. Why hadn't she? Her instincts, usually so sharp, had been sleeping.

'I can see it clearly now,' she went on. 'The pot pourri bowl that was smashed to pieces—I noticed it missing the day after Dominic Gray called. I remember now… he asked if he could use the bathroom and I showed him the way, and then went back to the kitchen. He could easily have followed me downstairs and slipped into the dining room without my knowing. I had the kitchen door closed, too. It was particularly cold that day, and he must have walked past into the courtyard, smashed the bowl and tipped the pieces into the dustbin. And I didn't hear a thing.'

'Why would you? You thought he was in the bathroom.'

'What an idiot I've been. The wasps in Leo's wardrobe—I was attacked the day after Gray had supper with me. I actually fed the wretch! He made some excuse about going to Leo's study to find papers for Mr Harker. Now I know where else he went.'

'He sounds a horribly devious man who deserves whatever Archie meted out to him.'

'I wonder what that was exactly? I heard him fall, I think, but I didn't see. I was on that parapet, facing the river.' She stumbled into silence, while Rose held her hand more tightly.

After a while, Nancy said suddenly, 'He thought Archie was living in the house! Or a man, at least.' She delved back into memory. It was strange how things that had been so blurry at the time were now crystalline. 'He looked at Archie's cardigan as though he'd never seen a cardigan before. It was because he thought someone else was living with me. Someone who might defend me from whatever March was about to inflict.'

'It's good to think it through, Nancy, but not to dwell on it,' Rose advised. 'You'll drive yourself mad otherwise, worrying over what you should have done. But it's with a second sight that you didn't have.'

'You don't know the worst.' She looked down at the starched counterpane, unable to meet her friend's eyes. 'I've given that dreadful man a blank cheque. Can you believe that? He could be emptying my bank account at this moment. Emptying Leo's account!'

'Not if the man is lying in a hospital bed,' Rose said practically. 'Maybe I can find out for sure if he was the one the ambulance crew went back to the river for.'

'If you could. And could you telephone the bank? It's the Westminster in Baker Street. Tell them what I've done.'

Rose was back in half an hour, though to a dozing Nancy it seemed only seconds.

'I managed to catch the crew on their break,' her friend said cheerfully. 'Luckily, they were the same men who were on duty yesterday. An hour after they collected you, they were called back to the river, to a spot close by. They were laughing about it, saying they should park the ambulance there permanently, then they'd save on petrol. Apparently, it was someone out walking their dog who found a badly injured man and telephoned for help.'

Nancy struggled to sit up. 'Gray? Was it Gray?' She was desperate to know it was.

Rose nodded. 'I wheedled his name out of the nurse on the men's ward. He's suffering from concussion and won't be going anywhere for a while.'

'And the bank?' Nancy asked, her face set.

'Nothing to worry about. The bank has stopped the cheque. They were very guarded in what they said, but I don't think they'd have paid out money, in any case. The transaction was too suspicious.'

Nancy sighed. 'So Gray was as stupid as me—to think the bank would accept his story.'

'Even stupider, daring to take you on!'

'Daring to take Archie on,' she said quietly.

'The nurse said you'll be well enough to leave tomorrow. I've arranged for the girls to go to Mike's mother and we'll drive up and collect you. The van isn't too comfortable, I'm afraid, but it will get us home.'

'You still want me to stay?'

'What kind of question is that? You're staying with us for as long as you want!

# Chapter Eighteen

## Hampstead, four months later

Spring had arrived in all its splendour. When Nancy looked out of her kitchen window at the square of garden behind the cottage, it was to see the pansies she'd planted when she first moved in, mingling now with a scattering of iris and delphiniums. The sun was slowly emerging from early morning cloud and she decided to take her breakfast tea outside, to the paved terrace below the kitchen window. A blue metal garden table and slatted chairs purchased from the local ironmonger had made the space a snug retreat.

Gradually, the house was taking shape: rooms decorated and possessions organised, the storage boxes opened one by one. Only the bedrooms were still in need of attention. She'd hoped to finish decorating before she left for Cornwall next week, but there wouldn't be time. Weekends never seemed long enough and she was too tired after a day in the studio to work in the evenings. The bedrooms would have to wait until she got back.

The memorial service was to be held the following Friday and Perry had insisted she travel down to Penleven several days beforehand. *It will feel strange for you to come here without Leo,* he'd said. *'You'll need time to get used to it before the ceremony.*

He was probably right. It would feel strange altogether to be returning to Port Madron. And difficult to be seeing Archie again—he would surely be there with the rest of his family.

When she'd left the hospital to stay with Rose, Nancy had written to him, a simple note thanking him for saving her life, as he surely had. It wasn't the first time, not for either of them. She had once saved *his* life, she reflected. When he'd replied, his letter had been brief, arriving the day Rose and Mike were to help her move to Hampstead. Archie hoped she'd recovered from her ordeal and thought she might like to know that he'd gone back to Abingers and asked to see Mr Harker, to tell him exactly how Dominic Gray had come by his injuries. Harker, Archie wrote, had seemed fazed by the details—who wouldn't be, Nancy thought?—but the whiff of scandal was enough for him to sack Gray on the spot.

*You won't be hearing from that con man again,* Archie wrote with satisfaction. *As for March, the enclosed cutting might help put your mind at rest.*

The cutting turned out to be a newspaper report that a man's body had been washed up at Tilbury. The body had been in the water for some weeks, the paper said, and identification was difficult, any documents long since washed away. There had been no reports of any missing person that might be a match, but the police had traced dental records suggesting the dead man had been a former journalist with the *The Daily Enquirer,* though the paper had not employed him for several years.

Nancy had felt overwhelming relief, breathing out deeply as she passed the article to Rose to read. Yet, there was also a grudging sadness. No one had reported March missing. No one knew or cared that he was dead. Not even her parents, for whom at one time he could do no wrong. The newspaper, for which he'd been so proud to write, had dismissed him as an employee they no longer knew.

'Well that's that,' Rose had said. 'Time to start your new life, Nancy. The car's packed and Mike is waiting.'

The new life was proving everything Nancy had hoped. She was once more absorbed in her work, travelling several miles every morning to the studio, and returning home every evening to a cottage she loved. At weekends, she shopped in the village and, when she wasn't decorating, took long walks on the Heath. It was a comforting routine. In a few months, though, the routine would change dramatically. She stretched herself against the iron chair back, stroking a stomach still barely rounded. Knowing her mother's history of miscarriage and her own miserable experience in Malfuego, Nancy dared not think too far ahead. But as the days passed and the sickness lessened, she'd begun to hope that this time she would make it to the end.

Once she knew for sure, she'd telephoned Rose, her friend almost bouncing down the line in happiness for her. But then there'd been a sudden silence, Rose breaking it at last to say, 'You have to tell him.' When Nancy made no reply, her friend asked anxiously, 'The baby is Archie's, isn't it?'

Of course it was Archie's. There could be no mistake. Leo had been sick for months before his death, and they had been friends rather than lovers. They always had been, she recalled ruefully, right from the start. That had been the problem. That and meeting Archie.

When, Leo had carried her over the Cavendish Street threshold after their marriage in the Fitzrovia chapel, Archie had been there, back early from a family visit to Cornwall. His expression had been unwelcoming, his gaze fierce. It was hardly surprising. All he knew of her was that she was the weeping girl his boss had once collected from Paddington Station and brought back to the house for tea and sympathy but now, after being away just seven days, he'd come back to find the weeping girl had become Leo's wife. He'd held out his hand to her, brusquely, unwillingly, but something had passed between them in that instant, something so viscerally strong that she'd pulled her hand back as though she had been burnt.

She hadn't told Archie about the baby and she was unsure she ever would. The pregnancy might come to nothing but, even if she were lucky and became a mother, he had made a new beginning for himself. He'd left behind the old life of which she was a part, and now that March was dead, he need have no fear for her. He could go his own way and leave her to do the same.

The path she'd chosen wouldn't be easy, she knew that well enough, though she was far more fortunate than most women in her position. She had money to cushion the difficulties she was bound to face, but social stigma was as powerful for the wealthy as for the poor. She could pretend the child was Leo's—the dates could just about be made to fit—but something deep inside her rebelled at the thought. People could assume what they wished, she decided, but if she were asked directly, she would be honest: *this child's father is a man I loved,'* she'd say, *and still love.*

Apart from Connie at work, Rose was the only person to whom Nancy had told her news. Her parents had no idea they might be welcoming a grandchild into the world. Ruth Nicholson had finally put pen to paper, but written only to scold Nancy for not returning to Riversley as befitted a young widow. What her mother would say when she discerned her daughter's changed figure, Nancy couldn't imagine. And her mother would. Harry Nicholson had telephoned last night—she'd felt obliged to give her father the new number, after her parents had continued their efforts to mend fences—

and made it clear that they wanted to attend Leo's memorial service.

'We never got to your wedding,' he said, 'but it's right we pay our respects to the family.'

'There's no need for you both to come all the way down to Cornwall. The Tremaynes know you wish them well.' Nancy had difficulty keeping the desperation from her voice.

'We've talked about it,' her father said complacently. 'And decided, your mother and I, it might be a good chance to have a short holiday. It's May and the weather has improved. And we've never been to Cornwall. We haven't been away for years.'

She was surprised to hear they'd ever been away. As a child, even a day trip had been too much for them. Wisely, though, she bit back the retort.

'I'm sure you'll enjoy the county,' she said diplomatically.

*

Perran Tremayne met her at Truro station, giving her an enormous hug as she stepped off the train. He looked a lot younger than when she'd last seen him, his face unfurrowed, his hair less scalped. He was dressed more casually, too, in corduroys and cotton shirt.

'I can't tell you how good it is to have you here,' he greeted her. 'It seems an age since I saw you last and such a sad occasion that I haven't wanted to remember much of it.'

'Nor me, but I'm glad to be in Cornwall. The memorial service should be less painful.'

He nodded. 'I've tried to make it a celebration. Chosen the hymns Leo and I sang as children in the church, and asked the people who knew Leo best to give brief speeches and the vicar to say one or two prayers. Then it's back to Penleven for a buffet—in the garden, if the weather holds.'

'It sounds just what Leo would have wanted,' she said, climbing into the passenger seat. 'It must have taken a good deal of time to organise.'

'I had assistance. Grace Jago is a marvel. She's been an amazing help in deciding the menu and shopping for it. She's kept the house spotless, too, *and* she has Dad completely under her thumb!'

'It will be good to meet her again.'

'You will. She's at the house now. I asked her to make a cake for your homecoming.'

The journey to Penleven took no more than half an hour and, as Perry brought the ancient shooting brake to a halt, the front door burst open and Grace danced down the gravel drive to meet them.

'Nancy, my luvver, it's wonderful to see you. And don' you look bloomin'?'

Nancy got out of the car and kissed her friend on the cheek. 'It's good to see you again, Grace.'

'Here, let me take the holdall. Perry, my luv, you take the suitcase.'

Nancy blinked. The last time she'd been here, it had been Mr Perran this, Mr Leo that, but Grace was now one of the family, it seemed, and it made Nancy glad. The gap between Penleven and the village needed closing.

'Don't forget your handbag,' Grace sang out.

Nancy bent to retrieve the bag she'd left on the back seat, her shift dress riding up slightly and for an instant outlining her figure. Grace fixed her with a look, her eyebrows slightly raised, but when Nancy looked steadily back at her, she picked up the holdall and carried it indoors, smiling to herself.

That was one more person who knew about the baby, Nancy thought. Grace had three children of her own, and inevitably her antennae were sharp.

'Kettle's on,' Grace said, leading the way to the kitchen.

'And the cake?' Perry asked anxiously.

'Take a look—chocolate. I remember Nancy loved it at Susie's party.' She busied herself setting out cups and saucers and reaching to a top cupboard for plates. 'Your Dad's 'avin' a nap at the moment, but 'e'll be in to say hello very soon.'

Gathered around the scrubbed wood table, the three of them made quick work of the cake, a large portion disappearing before Perran, still anxious, said, 'Do you think we've enough food for Friday? Several people have spoken to me today, people I didn't even know Leo knew, saying they were keen to attend.'

'My, you're a worrier.' Grace grinned. 'We've enough food ordered to feed the whole of Port Madron if they choose to come.'

'And your husband? Have you persuaded him?'

'Not persuaded, told 'im. Rich, I said, you are *not* takin' that boat out until after the ceremony. Steve and Lowen can't get 'ere, but Archie's comin' down. Well, 'e would, I s'ppose. Ma telephoned while you were away to Truro. He's down tomorrow and e's promised Ma to stay a few days, though she weren't sure 'e would. He's got a new job and that's provin' some busy.' She turned to Nancy. 'D'you know about the job?'

'I don't,' Nancy said. 'I haven't seen Archie for several months.'

Grace's eyebrows rose a little higher. 'Well, Archie's workin' with a Mr Simmonds at that auction house 'e was at. Mind, that were only temp'rary, but this is for good. Real responsible job, too.'

'Aubrey Simmonds?'

'That's right. Quite a name, innit? D'you know 'im?'

'I do. I once worked at the same auction house.'

Aubrey Simmonds. Nancy's mind was working fast. Archie must have taken Dominic Gray's old job. That was a neat twist. It would be interesting work for him and much better paid than the jobs he'd had since leaving Leo. She stored it away as something to talk about when she saw him at the memorial service, as she was bound to. It would help to deflect any questions she'd no wish to answer.

The sound of a stick tapping along the flagged hallway interrupted their conversation. Ned Tremayne put his head around the door. 'You've arrived, then?' he said, looking across the room at Nancy.

'As you see. How are you, Ned?' She had never brought herself to call him Dad.

'As *you* see,' he said sharply. 'Well enough. Good journey?'

'Fine, thank you, and Perry was at Truro to meet me.'

'Any tea going in that pot, Gracie?'

''Course. Sit yerself down, and I'll freshen it up.'

That was it, Nancy thought. The sum total of her father-in-law's conversation. She doubted there'd be many more words while she was at Penleven. Ned Tremayne was not going to change. He'd disapproved of his son's choice of a wife and he'd go on disapproving. Somehow, though, it no longer bothered Nancy. She didn't live at Penleven, she need never see the crusty old man more than once or twice a year – she'd do that for Perry's sake, if for no other reason. She had her own lovely home and, if she crossed her fingers tightly enough, she would soon have someone to share it with.

## *Chapter Nineteen*

Nancy woke the next morning to a shaft of sunlight pouring through cotton curtains that were thin with age. Grace hadn't yet got to grips with Penleven's outdated furnishings, but Nancy was sure she would. Perry was right. Grace Jago had become their saviour, running the house with efficiency and manoeuvring Ned Tremayne exactly where she wanted him. The thought of that cantankerous old man, stuffed with family pride, aloof from the village, being in thrall to a fisherman's wife, made Nancy smile. It was a joke she could have shared with Archie.

Tomorrow, she would see him for the first time in months, and no doubt they'd stand and chat for a few minutes with a glass in one hand and a vol-au-vent in the other, but then turn to talk to other people and that would be that. They'd moved on, she told herself. Both of them. If she ignored the ache in her heart, she could just about believe it.

When she went downstairs, Perry had already left for the mine and his father not yet emerged from his room. Unsure when Grace arrived for her day's work, Nancy set about tidying the kitchen before making herself a simple breakfast. She was washing up her cereal bowl when she heard a knock at the front door. Grace, she thought, though it was odd the girl didn't have her own key.

But it was Archie standing on the threshold.

'I thought you weren't travelling down until today,' she said, caught by surprise and stumbling over her words.

'I came last night. After Grace telephoned me.'

Confused, she gave a shake of her head. 'But why?'

He didn't answer her question directly. 'She told me you'd arrived. Shall we walk? You'll need a cardigan. It's sunny, but this early there's still a nip in the breeze.'

Archie was looking unusually smart in newly pressed trousers and a deep blue shirt that mirrored the colour of his eyes. It seemed to Nancy that he had taken control of the situation, talking to her as though they'd seen each other only yesterday, spoken to each other only minutes ago. She'd no idea what to make of it, but retraced her steps and collected her cardigan from the kitchen chair.

He was waiting for her on the driveway. 'Where to?' she asked uncertainly.

'I thought we might walk to the beach.'

Not any beach either. Nancy knew where he was headed. It was his favourite spot in the whole of Port Madron, the place they had first made love. A deliberate choice then, but why?

'I hear you have a new job,' she said, as they sauntered down the steep path leading to the beach. She needed to keep the conversation light.

'Gray's old job,' he said over his shoulder. 'Cunning, eh? But a good move for me.'

Nancy followed him onto the sand, soft beneath her sandalled feet. 'You're working for Aubrey Simmonds, Grace said.'

'Mostly, but Harker, too. He's an okay bloke. And the job pays well. It's been enough for me to leave Reardon Road and find something more comfortable.'

'I'm glad.' She paused, before saying, 'Has anyone at Abingers heard anything more of Gray?'

'Not a dicky bird.' Archie threw a stone into the sea, skimming it across the calm surface. 'I reckon he's done a bunk—to France. I remember he mentioned he had a cousin living in Lyons. Harker wanted to involve the police once he knew what had happened, but I persuaded him against. It would have dragged us both into court, and I thought it best to let it go. Hopefully, Gray will still be in a lot of pain.'

'What happened to him? I didn't see, but I guessed you knocked him out.'

Archie turned to her, a faint smile on his face. 'I did, but it was the way he fell that did for him. Cracked his head open on a paving slab. That will have given him a headache.'

'So he's gone… and Philip March, too, if that newspaper cutting is right.'

'Has to be. Did you ever suspect they were in league with each other—Gray and March?'

She shook her head. 'I didn't, but you did.'

Archie slipped off his shoes and she followed his lead, walking barefoot towards the water.

'Not really, though I knew Gray was up to something,' he said, truffling his feet through the sand. 'I'd no idea what or with whom. It was the phone calls I overheard—I didn't like the sound of them—though at the time, they didn't make much sense. Now, it's clear enough what he was up to. He was talking about *having it in the bag, then you*—he meant March—*can move in*, and later on, *we'll have to do it diffierently, I'll sort it out*. I reckon that's when March tried to break into Cavendish Street and failed. I did try to warn you what kind of bloke Gray was.'

'I know and I'm sorry.' She walked to the water's edge. 'Do you fancy getting your feet wet?'

'Why not?' He rolled up each trouser leg and followed her into the shallows, then pulled a face. 'I'm glad you didn't suggest a swim! The water's freezing.'

'Don't be chicken. It's refreshing.'

'It's certainly that. Tell me when you've had enough.' He splashed her legs with water.

'You shouldn't tempt me!' she said laughingly. 'But we best get back to dry land before we both ice over.'

'How did they get together?' he asked, following her out of the water. 'That's the question I've been asking myself. I know scum collects, but it's still a bit of a coincidence.'

'I can tell you that. I had it from Philip himself, and it was no coincidence. He went looking for the man—I think he must have seen Dominic Gray at Leo's funeral, noticed he was with staff from Abingers, and traced him back to the auction house. He decided that Gray could be useful to him, and he was. They had a deal. Gray was to get my money, and March was to get me,' she finished bleakly.

Archie held out his hand to her. 'Come on. Let's dry off.' Together, they walked up the beach to the cluster of rocks that enclosed the cove.

'It was clever of March,' he said, when they'd found a hollow in the warm stone. 'He was always good at tormenting you, but maybe he'd exhausted the strategy. Finding someone else to do it was a clever move. Someone who could get close, could taunt you, frighten you, without you suspecting.'

Nancy pursed her lips. 'And I fell for it. I'm not sure you're right, though. About Philip handing over his terror campaign to someone else. It wouldn't have been difficult for him to hurt me, even without Gray's help.'

'Too much of a risk, maybe. This time you might have gone to the police, and with a chance that you'd be listened to—Professor Tremayne's widow is a very different person to the friendless girl March originally persecuted. I think, too, that he wasn't sure you *were* on your own in the house. It's possible he saw Mrs Brindley leave in a huff, but maybe he thought I was still there. He needed someone on the inside to find out for certain. Gray was always keen to discover where I lived.'

'He might have thought you were still in the house,' she said slowly. 'He asked to use the bathroom once and he would have seen a man's razor and a second toothbrush. Leo's. It was a while before I could get rid of them,' she confessed, her gaze focussed on the white frill of a wave. 'And Dominic seemed transfixed by your cardigan. You know the one Leo borrowed and never returned.'

'One of Ma's colourful specials.'

'That's the one. It was draped across a sitting room chair.'

'So Gray could scout out the land for March, until he was certain it was safe to make a move.'

'Among other things, like breaking the pot pourri bowl and hiding the pieces. Like planting a nest of wasps in Leo's wardrobe. Softening me up for the kill, I suppose. By the time Philip came to Cavendish Street pretending to be a house hunter, he must have thought his path was clear.'

'I can see how March got what he wanted—luring you into danger—but how was Gray to get his reward? I know he was very short of money. Some pretty desperate characters turned up at Abingers a few weeks after the attack. They were looking for Gray, said he was in debt to them. He didn't get the money he was after, but why on earth did he think he would?'

'A blank cheque.'

'Signed by you?' Archie pulled down the sides of his mouth. 'He must have been pretty stupid if he thought the bank would cash a cheque for a large sum of money without first checking with you.'

'I wouldn't have been here for them to check, would I?' she said sharply Then shook her head. 'But you're right, he was stupid. And so was I. Believing his story of a new gallery that would showcase women artists. He was so convincing, though. Showing me the site, talking about the opening ceremony. He'd even had plans of the building drawn up. A great investment, he said. A great opportunity to do good… and I swallowed it wholesale. Like I say, stupid.'

'Just too trusting. Still, too trusting. You should have known better, after all we've been through. The sleuthing duo!'

It was the mention of the life they'd once shared that made Nancy decide. She slipped from her perch on the rocks, and stood facing him. The noise of the waves rolling to shore sounded loud in her ears but, taking a deep breath, she said what was in her heart. She hadn't meant to, but then she hadn't meant to be on this beach, and with Archie.

'I've missed you so much,' she said, not daring to look into his eyes.

'Missed, as in the past?'

'I miss you,' she corrected herself. 'And you?'

There was a painful silence until Archie said, 'Have we been idiots?'

'It's been hard—for us both. Leo was so unwell, then dying when I believed he was getting better. All the love and generosity he showed me—I never managed to repay it.' She felt the tears prickling. 'I felt I had to keep his memory alive in some way. I couldn't displace him.'

Archie slid off the rock to stand close to her. 'Would you be? You loved him as best you could. You cared for him through months of sickness. Do you honestly think he would expect more?'

'Perhaps not, but...'

'He told me in that Rio hospital that I was to look after you if anything happened to him.'

Nancy was astonished. Leo had been suspicious of their relationship, it had been clear, but Archie's words suggested that he'd known all along the true depth of their feelings. 'You never told me that.'

'Would it have made a difference?'

'It might have. Why didn't you tell me?'

'I couldn't, not when you were grieving for Leo. It was too soon.' He picked up another stone and skimmed it expertly across the waves. 'And I never really knew for sure what he meant.'

This time Nancy looked directly into his face, her gaze candid. 'It seems pretty clear to me. He meant that we should be together,' she said firmly.

'You think?'

Gazing into those startling blue eyes, she put her arms around him and pulled him as close to her as she could. 'Kiss me, Archie Jago.'

And he did. Several times and very deeply.

'There's just one thing,' he said, pulling back.

'What?' Her heart did a nasty jump. No more "things", she thought. Right now, she was too happy to bear disappointment. So happy she could have stripped off her clothes and danced naked in the waves.

He reached out and gently touched her stomach. 'This. When were you going to tell me?'

'Grace?'

'Grace,' he confirmed. 'It's why I travelled down overnight. But you still haven't answered my question.'

'I wasn't sure if I ever should. You'd started over, begun a new life, and this... complicates things.'

'*We've* started new lives, don't you mean? And how complicated is it?'

'You walked away twice and I didn't want to call you back again.'

'I'm not walking now, though, am I?'

'No, you're not, but I can't be sure it will happen,' she said quietly.

His eyebrows shot up.

'Of course, I'm sure I've a baby tucked in there, but for how long?'

He reached out again and stroked her stomach. 'It's a risk,' he agreed, 'but you seem to be doing better this time.'

'I'm crossing my fingers still.'

'Then we'll cross them together.'

'You mean that?'

'I couldn't mean it more.' Swooping down on her, he picked her up by the waist and twirled her round in a circle.

She was breathless and laughing. 'If you do that too often, we'll never uncross our fingers.'

'This time it's going to be okay, Nancy. What happened before... it's gone. It's past.'

'Like so much else,' she said, tucking her arm in his, and walking with him across the sand and back into the lane.

*

The memorial service passed off smoothly, every pew in the church filled, and afterwards a steady stream of well-wishers making their way up the hill to Penleven. Two long trestle tables, laden with food, filled the centre of the lawn and, in an attempt to make the garden look more attactive, Perran had bought a clutch of flowering pots to brighten the paved terrace at the rear of the house.

Grace, dressed in her Sunday best, a plate in either hand,

weaved her way through the groups of chattering people, while Perry, in charge of the drinks, followed behind. Nancy had seen a large number of bottles cooling in the refrigerator, but there was tea and coffee for those who needed a hot drink even on a day when the temperature was soaring. She caught sight of Archie's mother in the distance. Morwenna, busy as always, was replenishing the buffet from the Penleven kitchen, while Archie himself collected the empty glasses.

Nancy felt guilty that she alone was standing idle, but though it was a perfect day for an outdoor party, the sun having shone obligingly from first light, she felt herself beginning to wilt. The linen dress she'd chosen, another shift that masked her shape, was clinging uncomfortably. She had made no mention of the baby yet, either to the Tremaynes or her parents—they'd arrived late last night and were putting up at the Tinners Arms. *We don't expect to stay at the house*, her father had said. *We know the old man isn't well and we've no wish to be a burden on him.*

Or on me, Nancy thought. So far, she had barely spoken to either of them, but saw they'd found seats on the other side of the lawn. Very soon she would have to walk across and talk. But not about the baby, if she could help it. Time enough to share the news when Archie and she had settled their future together.

Morwenna was re-arranging plates on the table, trying to find a home for the last two trays of food. As soon as she had, she walked over to Nancy, her face creased in a smile.

'It does me good to see you, my luvver,' she said, enfolding her in a warm hug. 'How are you?' The older woman looked searchingly at her. Archie was sure to have told his mother the news, Nancy thought. If Grace hadn't got there first.

'I'm fine. Feeling the heat a little, that's all. How are you?'

'Doin' alright. A lot more time for my botany, now I'm

not workin'. And the grandkids are growin' up, not babies anymore, needin' all that attention. But you shouldn't be standin' around like this. Come and sit you down. Rest that back, though mebbe it's not so bothersome yet.'

'Not at the moment.'

Morwenna led the way towards a couple of rickety garden chairs that had been set out in front of the summerhouse and plumped herself down. 'I dunno where Mr Perran got these from. Ready to collapse, they feel.'

'Let's hope not!' Nancy gingerly lowered herself into the seat.

'Leastways, there're in the shade.' There was a long pause. Morwenna appeared to hesitate, but when she broke the silence, it was only to say, 'It was a good service today.'

'It was.'

'A curtain fallin',' she continued vaguely. 'A nice endin'. Kind of a resolution.' And Nancy knew she was thinking of her son's future and the future of this new grandchild.

There was another long pause, before she heaved herself out of the battered chair, saying, 'I'd best get back to the kitchen for a while. There's enough washin' up to last a month.'

Nancy jumped to her feet. 'You must leave it. Perry and I can do it later. You've worked so hard. Grace, too.'

'I can make a start at least.' Morwenna smiled down at her. 'And you need to take it quiet. Come and have tea with me tomorrow.'

'I will, I promise.'

Minutes later, Archie sauntered across the lawn and took the chair his mother had vacated. 'It was a good service,' he said, echoing Morwenna.

Nancy grinned. 'A curtain falling.'

'Was that Ma?'

She nodded.

'I can't stop her making plans, now she knows. I wouldn't have told her, but Gracie spilled the beans.'

'We didn't talk about it—not yet. But how does she really feel, do you think?'

'Bubbling. Wants us married this week and her new grandchild to stay as soon as he's born!'

Archie stretched his legs, shooting a quick glance at her. 'So… what about it?'

'Getting married?' Nancy laughed. 'To use another of your mother's phrases, it's kind of a resolution.'

'You can depend on Ma to have the right words.'

The crowd was beginning to thin and Nancy caught sight of Ned Tremayne holding court in a new deckchair bought for the occasion, respectful villagers on either side.

Archie had seen him, too. 'Doing his Lord of the Manor act,' he said tartly. Leaning across, he took hold of Nancy's hand. It felt like a statement of intent.

'Should you do that?' She'd seen Ned looking at them from across the lawn.

'It's Leo's memorial, not his funeral,' he reminded her, 'and I could have kissed you.'

'Ned will still be shocked and there's worst for him to come. What's he going to say when he knows his daughter-in-law is marrying a fisherman's son?'

Archie's eyes were laughing. 'It won't be repeatable. But who's going to tell the old curmudgeon?'

If you've enjoyed this novel, do please leave a review—a few lines is all it takes. It's helpful to readers and makes authors very happy (me included)!

*

Why not follow Nancy from the very beginning? See the whole series at:

US: **https://www.amazon.com/dp/B08GCZV4PW**
UK: **https://www.amazon.co.uk/gp/kindle/series/B08V88FHH3**

And follow me at **https://www.bookbub.com/authors/merryn-allingham** to be the first to know whenever there's a new release, pre-order or new discount!

# *FREE COPY OF THE DANGEROUS PROMISE*

Sign up to Merryn's newsletter and, as a special thank you, claim your FREE book.

*The Dangerous Promise* introduces Nancy Nicholson, the feisty heroine of the Tremayne Mysteries Series, setting her on a journey that sees her become an amateur detective and find the love of her life.

Merryn's newsletter is sent only when there is something special to communicate—such as new book releases, special promotions, and price reductions.

Click on the link below to be taken to the sign-up page. Your details will not be shared and you can unsubscribe at any time.

**https://merrynallingham.com/free-book/**

# *Other Books by Merryn Allingham*

*A Tale of Two Sisters (2019)*

*House of Lies (2018)*
*House of Glass (2018)*

*The Buttonmaker's Daughter (2017)*
*The Secret of Summerhayes (2017)*

*The Girl from Cobb Street (2015)*
*The Nurse's War (2015)*
*Daisy's Long Road Home (2015)*

Printed in Great Britain
by Amazon

41408440R00088